"A heartbreaking portrait of what it means to ⸺
violence trumps reason, and bad decisions begin ⸺
With wit, tenderness and intelligence, *Bull Head* exposes the raw
underbelly of male experience."

—Gary Shteyngart, author of *Super Sad True Love Story*

"John Vigna's prose grabbed me by the throat and wouldn't let go.
The characters in *Bull Head* never give up—they keep trying to fulfill
themselves by taking action. Like all of us, their decisions were the best
option at the time, but in retrospect often caused more difficulty and
damage. *Bull Head* is a brilliant book by a writer who never flinches."

—Chris Offutt, author of *Kentucky Straight*

"A remarkable ⸺ rd lives of
men and wom⸺ Vigna's eye
for detail, gift ⸺ e keys that
unlock these c ⸺ ccess to their
weary, yearnin⸺

—Richard Lange, author of *Dead Boys*

"*Bull Head* is full of yearning hearts, people living on the edge of trouble
and tomorrow. A man mourning his dead wife and daughters takes in a
vagabond gir⸺ ⸺ouches
toward their ⸺ble
landscape, fo⸺ ⸺ere
are gritty, he⸺ ⸺ and
feathery dust⸺

—Charlotte ⸺ auth⸺

"John Vigna ⸺ ⸺gside
complex hum⸺ ⸺out
making us de⸺ ⸺e
rich, compelli⸺ ⸺ prose
without prete⸺

—Steven Gal⸺

BULL HEAD

JOHN VIGNA

Arsenal Pulp Press   Vancouver

ARSENAL PULP PRESS
Suite 101 – 211 East Georgia St.
Vancouver, BC V6A 1Z6
Canada
arsenalpulp.com

The publisher gratefully acknowledges the support of the Canada Council for the Arts and the British Columbia Arts Council for its publishing program, and the Government of Canada (through the Canada Book Fund) and the Government of British Columbia (through the Book Publishing Tax Credit Program) for its publishing activities.

This is a work of fiction. Any resemblance of characters to persons either living or deceased is purely coincidental.

The following stories have appeared in a different form in the following publications: "Fences" (originally appeared as "Two" in *The Antigonish Review*), "South Country" (originally appeared as "Hops" in *subTerrain*), "Two-Step" (originally appeared as "The Ballad of Big and Small" in *Grain* and *Cabin Fever: The Best New Canadian Non-Fiction*), and "Gas Bar" (*The Dalhousie Review*). The author would like to thank the editors of each of these publications.

Cover photograph by Michael Jang for Getty Images
Author photograph by Nancy Lee
Book design by Gerilee McBride

Printed and bound in Canada

Library and Archives Canada Cataloguing in Publication:

Vigna, John, 1965-
    Bull head / John Vigna.

Short stories.
Also issued in electronic format.
ISBN 978-1-55152-490-0

    I. Title.

PS8643.I355B84 2012   C813'.6   C2012-905202-7

For Nancy

... the man in the violent situation reveals those qualities least dispensable in his personality, those qualities which are all he will have to take into eternity with him ...

—Flannery O'Connor, "On Her Own Work"

Therefore, since we are surrounded by such a great cloud of witnesses, let us throw off everything that hinders and the sin that so easily entangles, and let us run with perseverance the race marked out for us.

—The Book of Hebrews 12:1

CONTENTS

TWO-STEP

I

ARLENE IS BOTH kinds of music: country and western. When she stomps toward Earl, kicking up sawdust across the worn parquet dance floor, faux gold rings curved around her liver-spotted fingers and aquamarine rhinestones hanging around her neck, sweat beaded above her painted lips, eyelashes done just so, he sees his own hurt in her. He turns away and orders a beer.

"Earl, gawddammit, you're late." Arlene slaps his back.

"Sorry, honey, I've been packing."

"Packing? Something you forgot to tell me?" She runs her fingers along the marbled snaps on his shirt, tugs on his bolo, stands on her toes to reach his broad neck. "I oughta lynch you for making me wait so long."

The first beer of the day is cold and goes down fast. The fiddles and Dobro are loud and bittersweet. They sting like she does.

"You can't hang an innocent man."

"Baby, you're anything but innocent."

He laughs, pulls her in by the doughy flesh of her hip, presses his weight into her, and rests his chin on her head. Her hair is sticky and stiff but it smells clean. "You oughta know."

"I wish I didn't."

He drains his beer and sets it down. Nods for another. "Can't we have some fun tonight?"

"Fun seems to be the only thing you know."

On the dance floor, Earl holds Arlene tight, her hand damp in his, the tips of his fingers firm on her spine. He smiles as he leads her; they slide in swirls of sawdust, float in and out of other couples, counterclockwise around the room to the twang of Don Williams. He twirls her like a tiny doll, her eyes wide, boots gliding and stepping, thighs and calves brushing in long strides. Their silver belt buckles click when they come together. He is not a religious man, nor does he carry a great deal of faith in himself unless a woman puts it there. An ache of sadness tugs at him when he brings her in close again and whispers that he's leaving in the morning, that he'll be gone for a few days to see his brother. And when she pulls away and stops dancing, he's certain he has already lived the best part of his life.

"You're full of surprises, aren't you?" She studies his face. "The lone wolf rides again. Well, suit yourself. But don't come crawling back to me again. I can't take a man whose favourite topic is himself." She spins around and leaves him standing alone while the other couples twirl close, sawdust rising and falling around him, lost in the dark lights of the tavern.

II

Earl gears down the '72 Ford pickup he borrowed from his used-car lot to read the sign: "You are entering a Correctional Services Reserve. Any vehicle or person on this site is subject to a search. No loitering or photographs."

Crisp autumn air rises over the gin-clear river, the valley laid out before him like a dark green bottle. He inhales deeply before he unlatches the glove box, pulls out a flask of bourbon, snaps the cap, and takes a long drink. Whitetails and mule deer dot the open patches; a stand of birch and alder gives way to pine, spruce, and fir. He prefers the meadows that appear suddenly in the dense swathes of forest, cattle lowing on land cleared by generations of hardworking folks. But it's getting more difficult to recognize true pastures from the greened-over slag heaps that pass for hillsides. Geese honk above him in a melancholy song.

In the prison parking lot, he takes another swig before he stuffs the flask in his chest pocket. He slings a duffle bag over his shoulder and carries three plastic sacks of groceries toward the main entrance. A large German shepherd paces back and forth in a fenced pen. Behind, neatly manicured lawns; two white gazebos stand placidly outside of the barbed wire fences. He enters the waiting room and sits down.

The week before his visit, he had asked Hammy if there was anything he could bring, just say the word, anything at all. Hammy requested two rollerball pens, nothing else.

"Why?"

"To write."

"Write what?"

"Stories."

"What the hell kinds of stories?"

"I dunno. Stuff. Social worker says it's to get in touch with who I am."

"Is it working?"

"Hell if I know." Hammy sniffed on the other end of the phone.

"But the ink makes good tats."

They talked once a week; Hammy called collect punctually at seven p.m. on Sunday nights. Earl made a point of being home alone before he went to the Northerner for a night of dancing and drinking. He looked forward to the calls even though they didn't talk about much. It was better than the smashed and incoherent calls at all hours of the night before Hammy was arrested. What shook Earl were the phone calls when Hammy would be coming down from a high, his voice raw, a whisper on the other end of the line. "Maybe it'd be better for everyone if I just disappeared." And then he'd hang up. Once Earl asked the operator to see if the call could be reversed; she replied that it could, and the phone rang unanswered. He tried the line again and again throughout the night even though he knew it was a payphone he was calling. He imagined a solitary booth on the edge of a parking lot near a gas bar, the phone's ring echoing across the gravel like a death rattle mocking him. He finally gave up, lay in his bed listening to the birds chatter as first light appeared, reached for a nitroglycerin tablet, placed his hand on his chest, and prayed for his breathing to slow. The phone rang and Hammy was on the other end, his voice brighter than before. Earl asked him if he had found a fix; Hammy shouted, called him a fat bastard who only thought of himself, then hung up. Earl poured himself a generous shot of bourbon, yanked the phone line out of the wall, and rested the glass on his belly, studying the popcorn ceiling until it was time to get up.

Staring at a soft-drink machine in the waiting area, Earl feels the weight of his flask against his chest. He glances at the glass case on the wall jammed with trophies and banners and pictures of prison staff, smiling in softball uniforms, and considers turning around, getting a motel room for the night, checking out the local action in the bars, kicking up his heels.

"You waiting on someone?" From a booth lined with tinted windows, a guard with grape-coloured lips and a mouth packed with misshapen teeth emerges, blinking in the daylight.

"Here to see my little brother." Earl spells out Hammy's name.

The guard flips through pages on his clipboard. He picks up a phone, murmurs into it, hangs up, returns to the booth. A pretty, heavyset woman enters wordlessly, snaps on a pair of latex gloves, rummages through Earl's duffle bag. Her breasts push at the buttons of her uniform. Handcuffs jingle on her hip. She pulls out his nitroglycerin pills, pens, and flask. She digs through his clothes, yanks out shirts and briefs, shakes and leaves them on the counter in a heap.

"And this?" She holds up a crumpled naked woman, a deflated life-sized plastic doll.

"What else should a guy bring for his brother in jail?"

"All gifts must be registered."

"Let's register it then." He looks around, shifts from foot to foot, grateful no one else is in the room.

She drops the doll on the counter, makes a note on her clipboard. "Flask. Car keys. Wallet." She glances at his belt. "That, too."

He grins, slides the Leatherman and pouch off, and hands it to her.

"The belt, too."

"I like the way you think."

She dumps the contents into a small Rubbermaid bin and

drops it in a locker, locks it, and hands him the key. "They'll be here for you in three days."

"I'm looking forward to that." Earl stuffs the clothes in his duffle bag without folding them.

He walks through a metal detector. The guard pushes his bags through an X-ray machine, hands him a clip-on badge with a large "V" for "Visitor," buzzes him through two separate doors leading outside. The woman escorts him to a miniature house, a dreary slap-it-up-quick covered in the grey siding that characterized much of the company town he drove through to get here. A neatly clipped lawn and a waist-high chainlink fence surround unit B202, usually reserved for conjugal visits. A concrete picnic table sits bolted to the ground. Beneath it, a plastic pail is filled with sand and cigarette butts, a shovel jabbed upright in it.

"My tax dollars hard at work," Earl says.

"Don't make yourself too comfortable."

"How about a tour?"

She unlocks the front door and leaves.

He had expected bars on the windows, cots for sleeping, cold cement floors, metal toilets without seats, and bad-ass dudes at every turn. Instead Earl finds wall-to-wall broadloom, a large-screen TV and a boombox, a queen-sized bed, and a night table filled with packages of condoms. In the smaller bedroom there are two single beds with Bugs Bunny comic book sheets, a chalkboard, and broken sticks of coloured chalk. Nothing bolted down. It's a nicer house than he owns. He looks out the window; cameras pointed at all angles.

Another stocky woman, nothing to look at, strides toward the house. Hammy limps behind her carrying a small mesh sack. His hair hangs, stringy, receding; there's a triangular patch of fuzz beneath his lower lip. Despite the oversized T-shirt, Earl can make out his well-defined, muscular arms.

Earl offers a hand. "Hey, little man."

"Well, ain't this something? You showed up."

They embrace with one arm. The bones in Hammy's back and shoulder are sharp and feel brittle. Earl lets go and glances at his brothers face, pasty white, pockmarked with small scars, not clear and tanned as Earl remembered. Hammy's eyes jitter back and forth, marbled with red lines.

"You make sure you clean up after yourself and leave the house in the same shape you got it," the guard says. "You hear?"

"Yes, ma'am." Hammy keeps his head down as she walks out of the house.

"What's up with the women here?"

"To begin with, there ain't many, if that's what you want to call them." Hammy wanders through the house and stops at the children's room. "I'll take this one."

"No way, little man. Take the master."

"Nah, looks like you could use the space." Hammy chuckles, nods at Earl's stomach. "Hell, it'll just make it harder to go back inside, anyways."

"Suit yourself. I'm beat from the drive."

"Sleeping one off? That's all right. I'll be out here. I ain't going anywhere."

III

For dinner, Earl minces a head of garlic, sautés it in olive oil, and adds a can of tomato sauce. He simmers it for a few minutes, adds a pat of butter and a tablespoon of sugar, tosses in a pinch of chili flakes and serves it over a mound of rigatoni. His signature dish—Hammy's favourite. Earl watches him pick at his food. "Something wrong?"

"Nah, it's real good, Earl. I just can't eat spicy food anymore. Stomach can't take it."

"What's wrong with your stomach?"

"Nothing serious. Just these ulcers I got. The food's good. Nice to taste something with flavour compared to the tasteless crap they serve in there." Hammy flips his thumb toward the main building of the prison and pushes his plate aside.

"What's it like?"

"What's what like?"

"In there. What's it like in there?"

"What do you think it's like?"

"I don't know. That's why I'm asking."

"You're the smart one. You tell me."

"Must be tough, having to watch your back all the time, not knowing who you can trust."

"No shit, Sherlock." Hammy shakes his head. "That some lame-ass attempt to show you know something about what I'm going through?" Hammy stands and spreads his arms across the width of the table, checks to see if it's sturdy, then climbs on top.

"What the hell are you doing?"

Hammy pops the shade off the light, unscrews the bulb with his sleeve. "Just as I thought." He hands it to Earl. The bulb is hot.

"Huh?

"How many watts?"

"Forty."

Hammy lifts his eyebrows. "And?"

"And what?"

"Doesn't that strike you as strange?"

"No."

"Not sixty or a hundred?"

"No." Earl looks around the room. Even though all the lights are on, the room is dim.

"Try again."

"So guys won't electrocute themselves? So the prison can save money on their power bill? How the hell should I know?"

Hammy laughs. "When you start spending time alone, when your world is stripped down to its bare essentials, you get to see more clearly. It's the one thing I've gained in here. Clarity." Hammy screws the light bulb back in and hops off the table.

"I don't have a clue what you're talking about."

"Least you ain't lying."

"Does that make you feel good?"

"Yeah."

"What's the deal with the light bulbs?"

Hammy laughs again. "So we can't cook speed." He limps toward the kitchen, searches the cutlery drawer, pulls out a couple of jagged steak knives and holds them out. "Here, this might be something you can relate to."

Earl turns the knives over in his palm. The tips are blackened. It makes him nervous to hold the knives, sharp objects in the room that Hammy can access at any time. He places the knives back in the drawer, slides it shut. "Looks like high school all over again."

"There you go." Hammy smiles, leaves his plate on the table, and slaps Earl on the shoulder. "You bring those pens?"

"Yeah. You're not planning on smoking them or frying the ink or something, are you?"

"Nah. Not unless you want a homemade tattoo."

"I'll pass."

Earl goes to the bedroom and rummages through his bag. He lifts the doll, her mouth a ragged line. Jesus. Bad idea. He drops it in his duffle bag, grabs a four-pack of pens. He walks back down the hallway into the living room where Hammy sits in front of the TV. "Here you go. Twice as many as you asked for. Should keep you plenty busy."

"That's mighty generous of you." Hammy tears open the package, tests each pen on the back of the package and smiles. He opens his notebook and begins writing.

"Yeah, you're welcome for dinner, too."

IV

After Earl cleans the dishes, he watches TV with Hammy. The phone rings, startling them both. Hammy picks it up. "Hello?" He hangs up, opens the front door, and waves at the control booth. A flashlight flicks on and off, confirms he's been seen. Hammy sits down and turns to Earl. "So, why'd you come here?"

"Jesus, little man, how about a little foreplay before you bend me over and stick it to me?"

"Foreplay's a waste of time."

"Not in my experience."

"In here it is."

Earl meets Hammy's eyes; they flit side to side in quick

succession but remain fixed on Earl.

Hammy blinks and leans forward. "I know you, Earl. You're not here for the hell of it."

"Maybe I am. Is there anything wrong in that?"

"Who you running from?"

"Nothing. Nobody. I'm here for you."

"All of the sudden you're here for me, huh?"

"Sure. Why not?"

"Because you haven't changed a lick. You can't take your eyes off yourself anytime you pass a mirror. Hell, you were checking out your moustache in the reflection of the toaster while doing the dishes. Christ, you look like hell."

"Thanks."

"You drinking again?"

Earl glares at Hammy. "Not your business."

"I figured as much. But you're gonna lecture me on drugs this, drugs that, let me know what a mess I've made of things, tell me you'll always be there for me."

"Who's the one preaching? I don't need this crap, especially coming from you."

Hammy leans back into the couch, shakes his head. "Got it all sorted, huh?"

V

The brothers watch TV in silence until Hammy falls asleep. Earl wakes him, offers his hand to help him get up, puts an arm around his neck, and limps down the hallway with him, says goodnight, shuts the door.

"Leave it open."

Earl sits in the living room, flicks through the channels, the sound muted. His skin feels clammy. A headache pounds at the base of his neck. He wraps himself in a blanket but still shivers, turns off the TV, and sits in the dark; the silence rumbles in his ears. He could be back home now lying on the hood of his truck with Arlene, parked at the mountainside lookout, stars glittering above them, enjoying the murmur of her voice in his ear, her palm resting on his chest.

Earl gets up, goes to his room, and closes the door. The room glows with prison lights outside; there are no curtains on the windows to block it out. He rummages through his duffle bag and takes out the doll. It sags in his fingers. He stretches the plastic to unfasten the nipple and blows air into it until it's inflated and he can admire the full roundness of its face. It wobbles before him, eyes unblinking, mouth wide open as if in surprise. He listens to the quiet of the prison, lifts the doll in his arms, turns it around, examines it in the dark. Breasts like cantaloupes, legs all the way to the ground. It's young and has a firmer body than anyone he's seen or held in a long while. He turns it around so they face each other, and glides along the carpet with it. Quick-quick, slow-slow, quick-quick, slow-slow. He moves alongside the bed toward the door before spinning it around and, quick-quick, slow-slow, glides across the rug back to the other side of the room. Earl smiles, whether it's Arlene or Flo or Bonnie or even that crazy one, Millie, that he holds in his arms. He twirls the doll one last time before propping it up in the closet, resists a bow, closes the door.

He lies down panting, the sweat cooling against his shirt, his breath wheezing in the silence, a rasp that catches on something

22

in his throat on each inhale. He strains to breathe more evenly until he doesn't have to keep his mouth open. His chest rises and falls, the moments between each breath long and drawn. But he can't fall asleep. The light through the window, Hammy across the hall, the silence. He gets up, opens the closet, grabs the doll and lays it on its side, draws up the covers, and curls up behind it. The plastic skin squeaks against Earl's as they settle in together, and all is quiet again.

VI

The phone rings for count at seven a.m., jars Earl awake. His mouth is dry and his head pounds something fierce. The doll stares back at him. He rolls out of bed and stands it up in the closet, squeezes the sides of his head with his hands to relieve his headache, stumbles to Hammy's room. Hammy sleeps with his arms stretched over his head, bent at the elbows. In comic book sheets, Hammy looks like a child sleeping in on a Saturday morning, not someone hooked on meth and coke who robs handicapped elderly women. His fingers are smeared with black ink. After Hammy was born, their father lifted Hammy's tiny fingers, turned them over, sniffed, and announced to their mother, "Hands like a thief." The phone continues to ring. Earl shakes Hammy's leg. "Little man, you gotta answer the phone."

Hammy wakes with a stunned, guilty look, as if he's been caught doing something unpleasant and illegal. He leaps out of bed and waves to the booth, returns to his room.

Earl makes a pot of coffee and flops down on the couch. He drops his head forward and massages his neck, guides his fingers along the tight knots at the base of his skull. When he presses hard into one of the knots, nausea floods through him. He tightens his grip, turns his head and massages the muscle until his eyes tear, notices Hammy's notebook on the couch. Earl stops rubbing his neck, glances down the hallway before opening the journal, flips through it, dozens of pages filled with Hammy's handwriting, tight, thin spools of ink slanted hard to the right, but precise, fitting between the lines in each page of the journal. Stories about two characters, Big and Small.

Big and Small stand in a field, a gopher at their feet, a marble smashed in its jaw. The rodent makes shrieking sounds and snaps back and forth over their sneakers. Small dont want to cry because Big would beat the shit out of him. Small says: What if Pa finds out?

Big pinched the slingshot from the hardware store. Theyd have to do some explaining.

The gopher whimpers. Red and white bubbles grow and pop from its mouth and flies buzz around it. Small starts to cry.

Big says: Quit being a baby. Shut up.

Big gives him the slingshot and picks up a big rock. Big yells: Fuck you, motherfucker fuck fuck, and smashes the rodent into the dirt.

Big stares at Small. His eyes are hard. He says: flip it.

Small cant argue with Big, wont argue when he got in one of his nasty moods. Small pushes the rock away with his foot. The gopher lays crushed in the dirt, two teeth poke through a bunch of blood in the dirt.

Big says: Dont you dare say a goddamn word.

When they get home, Big narks on Small, tells Pa that Small pinched a slingshot and killed the gopher.

Pa slides the belt off his filthy jeans, smacks Small on the ear and pushes him into one of the horse stalls, slams the gate behind him. Small sticks his hand out, like always, and holds his wrist with the other hand and closes his eyes and tries to dream of a place far away but cant when the belt stings his palm.

Its not the killing, understand? Pa says, lifting the belt. Its the stealing.

Small hears Big on the other side of the gate, chuckling. Prays that Pa will hit him with the leather instead of the buckle as he had done before.

Earl slaps the journal down, slams the pens on top, leans back into the couch. That little bullshit artist. It wasn't like that. His leg trembles and his head throbs. He considers picking up the phone to call the guards and go back to his locker and have himself a little drink. Hell, he could leave. It wasn't like that at all.

Hammy wakes at noon and wanders into the kitchen.

"Made some coffee for you."

Hammy grunts, pours himself a cup and spits it out in the sink. "Still can't make a decent cup, can you?"

Earl listens to him open and close the fridge door again and again as though new food will materialize each time he opens it.

"Give it a break, little man."

"There's no food here."

"Like hell there isn't. There's a couple hundred bucks worth right in front of your nose, you—"

"You what? Finish your sentence." Hammy comes into the living room and stands before Earl.

"You could be a little more grateful is all."

"Christ, I'm grateful all right. You make me laugh. Lecturing me on being grateful."

Earl looks past Hammy around the room. The walls are grimy in spots. Workers walk past the unit, shovels on their shoulders, laughing in the sunlight. The fridge door is ajar, the coffee pot empty but the machine still on. "I'm getting some air."

"There you go. Run and hide. Nothing's changed."

"Shut the damn fridge and turn off the coffee machine." Earl goes outside, punts the plastic pail, and watches it sail across the yard and crash into the fence. He kicks over the toy dump truck. The workers have gone around the corner, but another wave of them sit on the back of a pickup, legs dangling off the tailgate. He reminds himself to bring Arlene flowers when he gets home; it seems like the right thing to do. He's not sure if she even likes flowers. He decides he'll bring her chocolate; what woman doesn't like chocolate?

VII

The drone of the TV fills the room as they eat dinner.

"You still dancing?" Hammy says.

"What?"

"Dancing. Two-stepping. Are you still dancing?"

"No."

"Why not?"

"What's it matter why? I gave it up."

"Why? No more room for all those trophies?"

Earl shakes his head.

"Then why?"

"Nothing." He feels the sting of his admission, another failure at sticking with something, and wishes Hammy would stop.

"Don't make sense to me, Earl. You were real good at it.

Made you happy. Or at least it seemed that way."

"Didn't have time no more. Not like you."

Hammy pushes his plate aside, leans his forearms on the table and laughs. "Least I'm committed. Do my time, don't hurt no one."

"Until you get out."

"The good Lord's keeping a watch on me. One day at a time, bro. I'm doing my best. That's all I can do. You might try it."

"The good Lord? Bad as any woman. Makes demands of you. Haunts your every move. Tells you what's right and wrong and punishes you for either, and then turns around and does whatever the hell He wants. Will let you down time and again, and if He don't, He'll expect something in return, something you can never give 'cause it ain't ever enough. Praise the Lord! Give thanks on ye, Lord! No way, little man. You hang onto Him, but the fact is, once you step outside of that fence, blinking like some dumb-struck lamb in the sunshine, standing in front of the pearly gates of heaven, you're gonna fuck it all up. Sure as snow in January. And where's He gonna be then?"

Hammy stops smiling. He closes his eyes and tilts his head back, his face colourless and slack, as if his jawbone has been unhinged. Earl fears his brother might start to cry. Hammy opens his eyes and stares at the light bulb on the ceiling he had taken down when they first arrived. He takes a deep breath and tips his head forward to look at Earl. His eyes are damp, but still.

"You know, Big E, the good thing about getting reacquainted with your own people is that you learn some new things about them, and you get to remember the old things you liked."

"I was out of line."

"There's nothing I can do about the past. Can't think about it, gotta move on, and live one day at a time." He leans forward. "I try to look for the good and positive in everyone, including myself. Hell, it ain't easy. You should give it a shot, too."

"Sounds like your social worker's been doing a tap dance on your head."

"Maybe. I dunno. It's better than the alternative."

"Which is?"

"Anger. The bastard child of being all alone."

VIII

Hammy scribbles in his notebook, chuckles to himself.

"What's so funny?" Earl says.

"Huh? What? Nothing."

"Tell me."

Hammy lifts his head. "Yeah, everything's about you." He taps his pen against the page and continues writing.

Earl gets up, grabs the remote, flicks through the channels. Two men fish on a calm stretch of water. He increases the volume. Water splashes over the gunwales as one of the men whoops and shouts at a halibut that thrashes around in the boat.

The men try to grab the fish, but it's too big and wriggles out of their hands, flops around the boat deck like something possessed. They try again, but the fish thrashes more violently. One of the men holds a blunt bat and beats on the halibut, sometimes hitting it, often hitting the deck instead. "Careful, keep back of him," his partner says. He flogs it again, but the fish twists viciously to the side, and its tail cracks the man's ankle, chops him to the deck. His partner reaches for the pistol on his hip, pauses for a moment, and shoots the halibut in the head.

"Damn," Earl says. "Now that's a fishing story."

"Dumb asses. They got horseshit lucky. What if they missed? Then what? They'd sink like a bucket of rocks." Hammy closes his book. "Find something worth watching."

"It's not like there's a whole lot of options."

"There's a few."

"None any good."

"Ah hell, just pick something."

IX

After Hammy goes to bed, Earl reads through his journal.

Big boxed with Stinky when they were eleven. Small hung around, wanted to watch, asking questions bout the fabric on the gloves, whats inside them, why so many laces.

Stinky was taller than Big and Small and he had grown up with two older brothers who took turns beating him. He said: Whats up with Small?

Big said, Get lost.

Stinky said: He can stay. But he cant just take tickets. Hes gotta fight.

Small felt his face grow hot. He smiled. Big locked the barn door.

Stinky shook his head and smirked. He said: Just dont go crying when I beat you to a pulp. He threw Small a pair of gloves.

Small pulled them on. Stinky circled, looking for an opening. Smalls first punch surprised Stinky, landed on his forehead.

Stinky said: Christ.

He rushed in and swung at Small but Small blocked the punches and hit Stinky hard, stopped him cold and opened a small cut above his eye. Stinky wiped it, glared at Small and bellowed: Okay, you little shit. That's it.

Stinky charged him, screaming like a cat in heat, battering Smalls body and head.

Small tried to catch his breath but the punches kept on. He felt his face snap back and found himself on the ground twisting around in the straw, the stench of horseshit all around. He heard Big say: Hes okay.

He knew Big was pleased he got knocked out because he could hear it in his voice. He knew it only proved to Big that he couldnt play with him and his friend and hold his own. Small felt Stinkys hands pull him up by the armpits and when he stood, his legs felt like jello. Stinky pulled off his gloves.

Stinky said: He should lie down. We need to get him some ice.

Smalls eyes watered and the skin above his eye throbbed. It would turn into a bruise. But Pa wouldnt notice and if he did hed only call him a goddamn pussy for getting his ass kicked.

Big said: Serves him right.

Small wobbled into the house, straight to his room, up the ladder to his bunk above Bigs.

Stinky said: What if hes got a concussion or something?

Big said: Hes fine. Hes just got a little headache.

Small lay curled, holding the blankets over his head. He heard Stinkys voice: If you need anything, let us know right away, ya hear? Youre a tough lil guy. You did good.

Small heard the light click and Stinky say to Big: Its a good thing he didnt fight you. Hed have kicked your ass.

Earl's hands shake. He sets down the journal, wipes his forehead, and sinks his fingers into the folds of the flesh on his neck to feel his pulse, faint but rapid. He takes a deep breath and exhales, closes his eyes. When he opens them, Earl clicks off the TV and goes to his room, shuts the door. The doll stands upright in the closet. Earl's hand squeaks against the puffed-up plastic of its wrist. He leads it into the room, to the foot of the bed, whispers in its ear, "Step together, walk, walk." He holds it in position and starts. Quick-quick, slow-slow, quick-quick, slow-slow. In the darkness, he dances with Arlene, holds the doll tight in his arms, spins it, his socks shuffle on the carpet. The doll's smile radiates inside him and he moves in the cramped space of the room, reminded of what he loves about two-stepping, the contact between two warm bodies, how both partners move together close in the most efficient and graceful way. He opens his eyes, stops to listen, but there's no sound. Peers out the window, the camera's gaze directly on him. He slides deeper into the room, near the closet, hums their favourite Willie Nelson song, "Georgia on My Mind." Earl considers what will become of them, him and Arlene, but the wondering makes his pulse accelerate, and when he opens his eyes again, he stares at the gaping mouth of the doll. Just one more night, he tells himself, plotting his drive back home. He'll start with some Chardonnay to sweeten the palate, move on to rye and coke. Beers in the cooler behind his seat, a cold can resting between his legs to steady him until he gets back to the valley. Hammy coughs across the hallway. Earl places the doll on the bed, undresses, climbs in beside it, and pulls the covers over both of them.

X

Earl wakes Hammy when the phone rings. Hammy answers, goes

back to bed. Earl picks up Hammy's journal, sips coffee outside in the sunshine. He's got a ferocious headache, one the coffee won't fix, no matter how many cups he drinks. The German shepherd barks and chases after a tennis ball that a guard tosses for him. Earl skims through a bunch of stories and stops at a list.

How to steal and never get caught:

1. Wear baggy clothing. Army surplus pants work best cause theyve got lots of pockets.

2. Pick the right store. The Bay is good (tho I got caught there once when I was too high) cause theres no undercover guards. Plus theres tons of small shit you can pinch and unload quickly on the street. CDs, watches, jewelry, that kind of stuff.

3. Scope out security. Most cameras are out in the open, hanging down in the corners of the store. Others are behind one-way glass. Avoid stores with armed guards.

4. Smoke and mirrors. You got to make sure you get near the thing you want to take but let it be. Pick up the thing next to it. Hold it up in the light, turn it over as though its the most important thing you need. While this is going on, grab the thing you really want with your other hand and slip it into your pocket.

5. Escaping. NEVER RUN! Keep cool and walk out as normal. If you get caught, pretend youre telling the truth. <u>Convince yourself and you will act innocent!</u> This is 100% foolproof in crime and life!

When Hammy wakes, he nods to Earl, fills his coffee cup, and takes a sip.

"Real good, Big E."

Earl pauses before answering to see if Hammy's sincere.

"Customized coffee for my little man. Nothing but the best."

Hammy sits down. He's in a good mood, more relaxed, and wants to fill Earl in about the prison band he's the drummer in, "Bitches Crew." The lead guitarist is also in for drug-related charges. They have plans to go out east when they're released to cut a CD and tour. Hammy's excited; Earl can hear it in his voice, the promise of something better. He didn't know that Hammy played the drums or any other instrument.

"Wanna hear us play?"

Earl considers it for a flash, knows there's only one answer; there's no way they'll make the trip out east—it's just a ploy to keep them going while they're doing their time, even if Hammy's telling the truth. "Sure. Just let me know when."

"No time like the present. Here's a few songs we recorded ourselves in the music room. Your tax dollars at work." Hammy pulls a CD out of his mesh bag, slips it into the boombox, turns up the volume.

The assault of metallic noise lacks any sense of rhythm or melody, caterwauling guitars, indecipherable vocals. Earl tries to listen. Hammy nods his head, moves his arms as though he's beating the drums. Despite the violence of the music and the drum line, he's calm and keeps good rhythm.

"Dance for me, Big E. C'mon, show me those crazy moves of yours." Hammy plays on, nods his head, his foot thumps the bass drum. His eyes are closed and he looks happier than Earl has seen him in years. "C'mon, Earl. Loosen up, bust a move."

"Sounds good, especially the drumbeat. But it isn't exactly dancing music, is it?"

Hammy opens his eyes. The joy drains from his face. He stops playing. "You're a bullshitter if there ever was one. I don't know how you do it or who buys it, but you are one certified bullshit artist." Hammy turns off the CD, shakes his head. "You disappoint me." He goes outside for a cigarette.

Earl sees him light up and exhale against the deep blue sky, pace the small yard, barking out fuck yous. He sits down on top of the picnic table, his back to Earl, faces the waist-high fence that surrounds the house near the taller brick walls of the prison. Earl reaches for Hammy's journal.

Big and Small and Mother stood on the front porch of their house. Small got caught with a baggie of pot. Pa was in the bush, two weeks on, one off. Both Cops had their hats in their hands. Skinny Cop had a neatly trimmed moustache. Fat Cop had grey hair. Skinny Cop said: Where did you find this? Small said: In the playground. At the bottom of the slide. In the sand. Fat Cop said: What were you doing there? Small said: Playing, what else would I be doing in a playground? Skinny Cop glanced at Fat Cop and said: Was anyone else around? Small said: No. Skinny Cop held the baggie. The contents were bright green, it was nearly empty. Small wondered how Big had found his stash, what hed done with the rest of it. Fat Cop said: Anything else we should know? Small said: No. Small was high tho, and the Cops were freaking him out. He was pissed at Big and would get back at him somehow, someway. Make him pay for this. Small said: Im telling the truth. Why dont you believe me? I told you I found it in the playground. That's the truth. Why wont anyone believe me? Fat Cop said: No ones saying otherwise. Fat Cop nodded at Mother and said: Its disturbing to think what would have happened if some little kids had found it. Small looked at Big, at the way Big glared at him, his fists clenched at his sides, silently goading him not to say anything else and knows if he did rat on him, that there'd be consequences to pay when Pa got home.

Earl's forehead is damp, his heart races. He runs his hands through his hair and pulls at the roots, trying to ease his headache. Lying comes easy to Hammy; he's hardwired to believe his own lies. Earl feels disgust at this thought; the tendrils of it work their way into him. He gets up, blows his nose, rehearses a story about having to go home right away, anything plausible to get out of the unit, out of the prison, back to his real life. But the idea that he is lying to himself right now, that he may be lying to himself unaware, unsettles him. He punches the sofa seat. "Goddammit."

Hammy comes back into the house, sullen and quiet, his movements weary and lethargic. Earl sinks back against the couch, his head heavy against the top of the faux leather.

Hammy sits down, scribbles in his notebook, turns on the CD, cranks up the volume.

"I might be getting older but I'm not hard of hearing."

"Remember that ewe we once had?" Hammy said.

"We had a lot of ewes."

"The one we left alone to graze in the tall grass in that fenced-off patch beside the barn?"

"Nope. But I remember a goat we had. He kept eating Ma's laundry off the line. We had to keep raising the line, but he'd still manage to get at it. That damn goat had skills."

Hammy grinned. "We left her alone and she ate and ate, as if she were trying to eat all of the grass around her. But there was a lot of grass. She was the fattest ewe I ever saw. After a while she couldn't even move except to bend down and graze. Just stood there eating. Her belly dragged on the grass she'd finished eating. When we sold her, we had to lift her into the truck by a harness and a tow truck."

"What's your point, little man?"

"She was never hungry. She gorged herself because she was always alone."

Earl stands over Hammy and forms a fist in his right hand. He clenches Hammy's arm, his fingernails dig into the flesh of his bicep. "Dial it down a notch, all right?"

They stare at one another. Hammy lifts his pen and hits the air as though with a drumstick, in perfect timing of the song's closing flourish.

Earl lets go, punches Hammy's shoulder. "Still sounds like shit."

XI

On their last evening, Hammy goes to bed early, jams his journal beneath his armpit. The TV on mute, Earl listens to the silence in the prison, the images from a movie he does not recognize flash on the walls. He watches without interest and drifts into sleep.

"Earl, c'mon, git up." Hammy tugs on his sock. "Still falling asleep in front of the boob tube, huh? C'mon, git up. You got a long drive tomorrow."

Earl opens his eyes to find Hammy hunched over him. The last time Hammy woke him up was over a decade ago. He had a rifle across his lap, his breath reeked of booze and snuff, and he suggested they hunt squirrels in the middle of the night. Another time he had leaned into Earl's face and in a quiet, menacing tone told Earl that he had slept with Earl's first wife, that she'd been "gagging for it." Now, waking Earl on the couch, Hammy's gentleness terrifies him. Experience has taught Earl it's dangerous to believe in what another person seems to be. They will always surprise you. They will always let you down.

"You're a good man for coming here." Hammy offers his hand. Earl grips Hammy's hand to lift himself off the couch.

"You're all I've got left." Hammy holds his hand tight. "The only thing that's real. I just want you to know that."

"Maybe I'll come back, pick you up when it's time to get out of here." Earl feels good in making the offer, but realizes he's just uttered what Hammy predicted he would say. He lets go of Hammy's hand.

"That'd be nice, Big E."

"You know what I mean."

"Yeah."

"'Night." Earl stumbles down the hallway to his room, closes his door, glad to be alone.

The doll lies crumpled on the closet floor. He lifts its limp body, unclasps the valve on the nipple and blows into it. Air hisses out of its neck. He blows into it again, but it's no use, the air doesn't take. He examines the rip; it's torn along the edges as if slashed. A black-tipped knife lies on the carpet. He drops the lifeless plastic, pushes it aside with his foot, closes the door.

Earl crawls into bed, the camera outside trained on him. He turns on his side and tries to sleep, but can't calm himself. Each inhale comes in short, shallow bursts, his chest feels clenched. He counts each breath, exhales slowly, not now, dear God, not here, not now. Hammy tried his best, was still trying his best, and Earl regretted not being a better brother to him, rather than avoiding him like he was a damaged gene that might infect him. It occurs to Earl that Hammy might be avoiding Earl for the same reasons, that he sees Earl as the damaged one. Earl gasps for air with his mouth open, a hoarse rasping shallow in his throat like some old man taking his last inhalation. He exhales slowly, draws another breath until gradually his panting subsides. He'd pick up Hammy when he was released, help him get his feet on the ground, let him stay at his house for a while. But as his breathing returns to normal, he knows these are just thoughts to help himself feel better. He would have to keep Hammy away from Arlene, that much was certain. Earl would see Hammy whenever he decided to show up, probably when he was broke again and had hit rock bottom. Earl had done his duty by visiting him. That counted for something.

XII

In the morning, the phone rings early for count. Earl wakes Hammy. After Hammy hangs up the phone, he mumbles, "Fuckin' screws." Earl grins.

Hammy does not go back to bed. Earl makes him coffee and they sit on the couch in front of the TV. Hammy turns it off, holds his journal, flips through the pages. "You all right, Big E?"

"Yeah, fine. Why?"

"I worry about you."

"There's nothing to be bothered about. If I have any worries they aren't anything like what you've got."

Hammy looks him in the eyes and smiles. "Sure. A man can

38

get whipped but that don't mean he's beat, right? Glad you're doing well." He turns away. Two guards walk toward the house. "They're early." He taps the journal against his thigh. His voice is low, barely a whisper. "Big E, I don't want to go back."

Earl nods, glances toward the guards approaching, uncomfortable with Hammy's confession. He considers the attractive guard from the first day. Maybe he will hang around town for another day or two, get a room, see where it all leads.

"Can I ask a favour?" Hammy says.

"Depends."

Hammy hands him the journal. "Can you hold this for me?"

"Why?"

"Safekeeping. It'd just get stolen or trashed in here."

The short stocky woman Earl saw when he first arrived opens the door to the house. Even after three days, she's not much to look at. "Ready?"

"Yes, ma'am, in a minute." Hammy gathers his things, stuffs them in the mesh sack. Earl's bags sit packed by the door.

"So, will you?" Hammy says.

"What about your social worker?"

"It's time to start another one."

"Sure. Of course."

"I'd tell you not to read it but that'd only make you want to read it. Hell, it don't matter to me. It's all true. Stories about my life. I got nothing to hide." He looks around the room, nods to the guard, shrugs. "Seriously, where am I gonna hide?"

Hammy hands Earl one of his prison issue T-shirts in exchange for one of his. They pull them on. Earl's shirt hangs loosely on Hammy, the neck too wide; the bottom of the shirt drapes below his waistline. Earl struggles against the tight fit of the cotton from Hammy's shirt. He stretches out the bottom in an attempt to cover his belly and folds his arms over his chest, but air hits the flesh of his stomach so he pulls down on the shirt and exits the house with Hammy. The guard locks the door, shuts the gate.

"Worried about a break-in?" Earl says.

Hammy laughs.

They shake hands in front of the guards and cameras and prison-yard workers.

"We can't help who we are or what we've done. We just have to keep trying to move forward, right?" Hammy's eyes dart back and forth; he gives Earl an everything's-a-okay smile. "I sincerely wish nothing but the best for you, Big E." He turns and limps toward the main part of the prison, one guard in front of him, another behind him, his mesh bag of belongings slung over his shoulder, Earl's T-shirt baggy on him; a little boy being sent off to summer camp.

Earl stands alone in front of the prison, unsure of what to do next, where to go. "Hey, Hammy," he shouts out. "Wait a sec."

Hammy does not look back.

SHORT HAUL

I

FRESH MEAT FRIDAY, the bar crowded with men from all over the valley who have come to see the new lineup in town. As Lonnie squeezes into a chair next to Ricky, the men behind him murmur that they paid good money for their seats, sit the fuck down already. They hunch over low tables, pink fleshy mouths gaping like wounds, dirty boots, fading mack jackets, and ball caps pulled down low. Sausage fingers pinch the necks of their beer bottles; eyes blink dull and dim, gawk at the stage. Beneath a mirrored ceiling of red, black, and blue spotlights, the stripper is down to a policeman's hat and PVC thong. "Dirty Laundry" booms through the bar. Ricky clamps his arm around Lonnie, tells him to ignore them, orders another round of overpriced Jack shooters, chased by the beer special.

"Whoo-hee! If she's not the hottest cop I've ever seen." Ricky leans forward, his tattooed arms and sharp elbows splayed on the stage.

The stripper swings from a gold pole by the crook of her arm. Her hair spills down her back like sun-bleached barley, silver anklet twinkling in the lights. She pivots on five-inch heels and squats, crushes her inflated breasts together, pretends to lick the length of the brass pole. The room grows rigid, a collective holding of breath, so silent that Lonnie hears the woman's skin squeak against the pole as she lowers herself and crouches before him. Ricky and the men behind him exhale a low, hoarse whistle and for a moment Lonnie imagines a scent of sagebrush and pine needles, deep from the valley's farthest corners, instead of the cheap cologne and rank sweat of men around him, breathing through their mouths like dogs circling for scraps.

Behind the stage, a football game plays on the large screen. The Patriots complete a pass in their hurry-up offence. The stripper stands in front of Lonnie, pulls a finger out of her holster, takes aim at him, fires, and blows the tip of her French-manicured nail. Her green eyes stop on him, sum him up in a flash, and quickly dismiss him. Pass incomplete. Second down.

"Heard anything?" Ricky stares straight ahead.

"Nope."

The song ends and "All Out of Love" begins. The seats creak, men shift behind him. After three long dance numbers, the stripper circles the stage with her tattered Navajo blanket, one hand to her ear while men whoop and holler and wave.

"Right here, baby." Ricky thumps the stage with his palm and holds up a folded five-dollar bill. The quarterback scrambles for a few yards before he slips out of bounds. The stripper fluffs open the blanket, spreads it in front of them. Lonnie senses the men behind him lean forward, waits for one of them to pat his back in a sad, conflicted gesture of brotherhood that comes when men drink beer and watch naked women together.

"That's what I'm talking about." Ricky tosses the note on the blanket, slaps Lonnie on the shoulders. "House arrest, big man."

Fourth down. Lonnie shakes his head. The stripper slides

toward him on her hands and knees, stares at Lonnie with a look that could split firewood from a hundred yards. She holds up a pair of handcuffs. A silver key glitters from a thin chain on her neck. The men behind him yell, pound their tabletops with their fists. One of them taps Lonnie on the back, pushes him toward the stage. Ricky holds out his wrists and grins. She shimmies closer, sits on her heels and bounces up and down, pinches her nipples and tips her head back in a soft, well-rehearsed moan.

"Sentence me, baby. Give me life." Ricky pulls out another fiver and drops it next to her. She smiles and grabs Ricky's head, smothers his face against her chest. He gives the thumbs up and men yell, raising their drinks in the air. She pushes Ricky away and turns to Lonnie; with a pout, she reaches to touch his bad eye with her fingernail. Interception. Lonnie freezes; her face softens. He jerks his head back, stands, and marches across the bar to the door marked GENTS.

The toilet is empty, quiet. Back in the bar the men chant, "Shower, shower, shower." Ricky's voice croaks above the rest.

Lonnie looks into the mirror, examines the black and purple bruise spreading outward, thinning into jaundiced yellow. Another week and it will fade. He scrubs his hands with a cracked, filthy bar of soap. His gold wedding band is buried in the flesh of his finger, but grazes him when he splashes water on his face; he wants to drag the edge of it along his skin, scrape his face into something grotesque. Lonnie stands back from the mirror and sucks in his belly, pulls up his pants, cinches his belt a notch, but it only hurts his hip and makes his stomach look larger when he inspects his profile from the side. "You're not fooling nobody, lard-ass." He pinches the doughy folds of flesh, jiggles them in his fingers, imagines slicing them off to give himself the flat washboard look he convinces himself he once had when he was younger. "All Out of Love" starts again near the end of the song, an encore; the men roar and slam tables. Lonnie pulls his shirttails out and swings the door open.

Ricky waves a rolled-up poster at the waitress, points to his shooter glass, and raises two fingers. The stripper meanders between tables, leads a grey-haired man by the hand. Just a salesman, not a real working man, Lonnie decides. Her red satin housecoat pulled tight at the waist, she carries a bundle of clothes and her blanket, handcuffs dangling from her fingers. She offers Lonnie a weary smile. He stands aside; his butt pushes against the chair backs.

"See you around." She brushes past him. The old man follows, raises his eyebrows in a conspiratorial glance. They wind their way through the bar toward a doorway marked No Entry. She shoulders the door open, pulls the man in, and bumps the door closed with her hip.

Lonnie joins Ricky, grips his shoulder. "Sorry, bud, gotta go."

"What? Duos are next."

"See you in a few days."

"What the hell, big guy? I got shooters coming." Ricky taps Lonnie's stomach with the poster. "Christ, she's got you by the short and curlies."

Lonnie raises a fist as though to punch him. Ricky doesn't move.

"Hit me." They bump fists. "Later."

Lonnie glares at the men sitting behind Ricky. One of them lifts his bottle and sneers. "You have yourself a good night."

He leaves through the back, passes the No Entry door. At the edge of the parking lot, two does graze on pine needles, lift their heads, and scamper into the trees. He climbs into his rig, lights the diesel, reaches for a pack of bubble gum, unwraps two pieces, and pops them in his mouth to mask the stink of beer. He starts the engine, slips the truck into gear, and begins the hour-long drive home.

The fresh tang of summer dusk rushes through the cab window. The sky a dark sepia film, two ravens swim over the road, land on the shoulder and hop off into the ditch as Lonnie's truck rumbles toward them. He drives east along the Crow, built on the dry bed of the Elk River, cutting through the once sacred land of the Kootenai. Narrow valley bottoms crowded by the granite billows of sharp mountains. The sun drops off the horizon behind him, casts shadows over the eastern hills. These mountains are his home, not Dani's. She came to ski, and like many others, did not leave after the snow melted and the prairie crocuses sprouted up. As he clears the tunnel, Bull Head Mountain comes into view, towers over town, the postcard-perfect shadows showing a Kootenai Chief and his daughter on horseback, legend has it, chasing another man. It gives Lonnie the creeps each time he sees it.

He pulls up on the patch of dirt in front of his boyhood home. Spackled siding with shards of broken glass mixed in; faded porch boards in need of paint. The curtains are drawn, but the living room light is on. Next door, Johnson waters his garden, the embers of his cigarette glowing in the darkness. A glass of home-made plonk sits on top of Lonnie's low fence.

"Long day?"

"You know it." Lonnie stands at the rotting fence, careful not to lean on it. Another item on his long to-do list of repairs around the house. "We've been hauling near 120 Mile, Top of the World." Johnson's black and tan barks, strains against a short, frayed rope tied to the porch. The water dish lies upside down. Fresh mounds of dug dirt stack against the side of the house. Lonnie catches a whiff of dog shit.

"Cutting that far back now, huh?" Johnson shakes his head. "Hell, we used to cut near the front of the valley. The trips short and sweet. I'd get five or six in a day, take a dip in the hot springs and still be home for dinner and a tumble in the sack. Those were the days."

A lanky blond boy carries a stack of fresh poplar limbs into Johnson's house. Lonnie considers what he'd use them for, too green to burn. Another boy sits on the ground, pushes a dump truck back and forth, scoops shovelfuls of mud into the back of it and then tips it out. The third boy stands beside Johnson's leg, tugs on his belt loops.

"Hi, little fella." Lonnie reaches to tousle the boy's hair, but he turns away. The dog barks.

"Goddammit, shut that mutt up." Johnson turns to the boy, smacks him on the head. "Where's ya manners?" The boy stares at Lonnie. "They'll be the death of me," Johnson says. "Starting with her." Johnson nods toward his wife coming up the alley. She's heavy and bloated and carries two garbage bags rattling with empty cans and bottles. A small boy drags his feet behind her. "It's a race I got no chance of winning."

The dog pulls at its rope, its barks turn into high-pitched yips. Dani was right: the wife is pregnant again. Her theory that Johnson keeps getting her pregnant so they can collect child allowance from the government to supplement his disability cheques seems about right. Lonnie nods, but her face remains passive as she walks past them and enters the house. The little boy next to Johnson runs in after her.

"Jesse, shut that goddamn dog up."

Jesse pushes the toy truck, dumps another load of mud, and kicks the truck on its side. He slaps the dog's head with a plastic shovel. The dog yelps. Jesse lifts his shovel again. The dog cowers and whimpers.

Johnson crushes his cigarette against the fence and slides the butt into his cigarette pack. He takes a long guzzle from his glass. "I want to show you something. Gimme a minute."

While Johnson disappears inside his house, Lonnie studies Johnson's greenhouse, brightly lit, but covered with a thin black screen, making it difficult to see the leafy plants growing inside. Johnson has told Lonnie he grows tomato plants, but they don't smell like tomatoes. He comes out carrying a rifle, glances up and down the alley, cocks the lever-action.

"Check it out. 1892. Modelled after the gun that won the west." Johnson lifts it to his shoulder and aims down the alley. He pushes the rifle toward Lonnie. "Go on, take it."

"That's all right. It's a fine looking gun."

"C'mon. Try it. She pulls a bit to the left but she's honest. A real collector's piece." Johnson offers it with both hands. "Careful, she's loaded."

Lonnie takes the rifle. It feels lighter than it looks, makes him anxious, as if it could go off at any moment and change the course of his life. But what makes him more nervous is the knowledge that his neighbour stores a loaded gun in a house with a pregnant wife and five boys. That would be a deal breaker for Dani. If she found out, they'd have to move out.

"It's yours. Hundred bucks."

Lonnie shakes his head, hands the rifle back to Johnson. "I better get home."

"I'd do the same if I had a pretty little lady like yours. Eighty."

"You don't understand. It's not the money."

"A hundred then. It's still a steal. I know you're good for it." Johnson picks up his bottle and crosses the alley. "Sleep on it." He raises his glass and enters his house.

Lonnie walks across the yard, opens the door to his truck, slips the gun behind the back seat, covers it up with his Storm Rider, and climbs the front steps of his porch.

Inside, the house is warm and smells of chili. A wooden spoon rests against a plate next to the stove. He kicks off his boots, lifts the lid, sniffs, picks up the spoon and digs into the pot, blowing on the chili to cool it before taking a mouthful. An empty wine bottle sits on the countertop next to the toaster and coffee maker. He reaches inside the pot to get another taste.

"Don't stir with that spoon." Dani startles him, leans against the doorframe.

"I thought you were upstairs." He drops the spoon in the sink.

"You know I don't like it when you leave things in there."

"Sorry." He rinses the spoon and puts it in the dishwasher.

"Where the hell have you been?" She steps into the kitchen and rests against the counter, clenches her wine glass. Her brown eyes are narrow and steely; her dark hair wet, pulled back in a tight ponytail.

"I lost track of time."

"Where were you?"

"Out with Ricky."

"Where?"

"C'mon. It's Ricky. At the bar."

"The titty bar?"

"We had a beer after work."

"Jesus, I only ask one thing of you. One fucking thing." She smacks the fridge door with her palm.

"I only had one beer."

"I don't care if you had ten. You're so selfish, you know that?" Her voice wavers. "Do you have any idea how many of those women are abused, hooked on drugs? How can you sit there and watch them?" She wipes her eye with a knuckle.

"Sorry." He steps toward her.

"You make me sick. Don't touch me."

"It was just a beer. You know how Ricky gets."

"No. How does he get?"

"Listen, it's been a long day. I left him behind and rushed home. Let me fix you a drink." He uncorks another bottle of wine, fills her glass.

"You can be such an asshole."

"I know. I know." He massages her neck and shoulders.

"How's your eye?" She strokes the swollen skin below his eye with the pads of her fingers. Her touch feels strange, comforting.

"Makes me look like a bad-ass."

"Things have been so crazy at work lately."

"I know."

"It looks a lot better." She kisses his ear, whispers, "Does it hurt?"

"It's fine."

"Forgive me?" Her voice vibrates low in his ear. She nibbles on his earlobe, tugs it.

He wants to believe that she's turned a corner and, once the pressure of her work subsides, she'll be more like the woman he married three years ago. He nods. "Sure."

She pulls away and holds out her glass for him to refill, and when he does, she grabs a bowl from the cupboard and places it on the counter. "You better eat. Morning's coming fast."

II

The next day at Canal Flats, after he makes the first of three long hauls and waits as the loader plucks trees from his trailer, Lonnie writes a letter. His pen scrawls over the sheet of paper, a desperate man's scratchings.

His last personal ad went unanswered, but Ricky encouraged him to write another, and although he hadn't seen the letter, Ricky teased that it had been too serious, filled with too much horseshit. "You gotta stand out, man. Like a black wolf or a one-legged man in an ass-kicking contest. A guy with a patch over his eye, something. Make women take notice of you."

Now Lonnie tries to write something true about himself, something light.

Robust Romeo Seeks Shapely Juliet:
I'm a 34-year-old, overweight underachiever on the verge of giving up on love. I have short black hair and dark brown eyes. I pray when I need help and I'm embarrassed to say that I own a Bible but proud to say I haven't read it because frankly, it bored me to death when I tried. Guess

I'm going to hell. I'm somewhat athletic, or at least was. Now I sit on my butt all day and super-size my meals. I use Dial soap and sleep with my feet outside of the covers.

I drink but don't smoke and I'm not very good at being around strangers. Most of the time I'm lonely and moody. Plus, I'm married. She once loved me but now loathes me. Despite my spare tire, trucker butt and secret love of donuts, I'm what you might call a good-looking homebody.

He re-reads the letter, folds and slips it into an envelope, addresses it to *The Free Press*. After the logs are unloaded, he drives to the general store in Canal Flats for a stamp, two cans of cola, a candy bar, and a large bag of potato chips. He slips the letter through the mailbox slot and begins the long drive to Top of the World, taps his fingers on the steering wheel, dips into the bag of chips between his legs.

III

Later in the week, after he drops off the last load of logs, Lonnie stops to check his post office box. He parks his rig behind Tamarack Mall, climbs down, and ambles past rusted low-ride sedans and shiny pickup trucks with dual rear tires.

He walks along the row of shops—Chatters Hair Salon, Sunshine Video, Saan. In Suds & Duds, he is startled to see the stripper standing in front of a washing machine with a young boy who holds a basket of laundry. She wears loose navy blue sweatpants short on the calf, tennis sneakers, an oversized sweatshirt. Her hair is tied up.

She helps the boy stuff some dark clothes into the washer,

dumps in a capful of liquid detergent, digs through her pockets for change. She's shorter than he remembered. Lonnie notices her anklet. When she glances toward the window, he freezes. They lock eyes for a moment before he turns away, scans the parking lot, kicks at the ground. He looks up again. She's immersed in a celebrity magazine. Her son slouches in a chair next to her with his arms crossed. Lonnie considers walking into the laundromat to pretend he's waiting for his laundry, buy a candy bar from the vending machine, casually strike up a conversation with her. But there's the grime on his jeans and hands, his suspenders, his sweat-stained ball cap. Instead he hurries into the card shop and checks his postal box. Empty. He leaves and stops in at the Overwaitea, buys two packages of steaks, a can of corn, four large potatoes, and a box of tampons for Dani, and rushes past the laundromat without lifting his head.

IV

The lights are off when he arrives home. Next door, the Johnson boys hammer boards together in the shape of a small dog kennel; Johnson shouts at his wife inside the greenhouse.

Lonnie closes the door and sets the groceries down on the counter. "Dani?" He kicks off his boots and climbs the stairs. "Hello?" Sits on the edge of the bed, peels off his wool socks, unhooks his overalls, unbuttons his shirt.

He turns the shower on and steps into the tub, draws the curtain behind him. Runs a bar of soap under his armpits, over his drooping chest, jiggles the flesh beneath each breast, pins his shoulders back to stretch the skin. Dani's right. Man boobs. He tries to recapture the stripper writhing on the blanket in front of him. Her legs spread open, her hairless skin, the way she touched herself, covered her crotch with the palm of her hand, her smile penetrating him. He tugs himself a few times but remains limp. Lonnie turns off the shower, towels himself and wipes the fog from the mirror. The bruise gives him a tough look, one he admires. "I'll kick your ass." He pivots away, then toward the mirror. "I'm not kidding. I'll kick your ass." He presses his fingertips on the sore bone beneath his eye, slides his finger along the length of it so the pad of his finger touches the lower part of his eye. He sucks in his stomach, sticks out his chest, squints into the mirror, punches the air in front of him. "What are you gonna do about it, huh?" His stomach hangs over his groin like a shaggy meat skirt. Lonnie turns away from his reflection and exhales with resignation. The door opens downstairs. He dresses and hurries down to meet Dani.

"Hey. How was your day?" He leans toward her, but she turns away, slips out of her jacket, sets down her backpack.

"Messed up as usual."

"Hungry? I'll get dinner started."

She looks at him for a moment. Her face is ashen, whipped. "Jesus, is that all you think about? Food?"

"I just got home. These long hauls are killing me." He takes the steaks out of the fridge, unwraps them, and seasons both sides with salt and pepper. Blood leaks around the edges.

"I suppose you stopped in to see Ricky?"

"I picked up the groceries, came straight home."

"Like I believe you." She looks in the cupboard. "Don't tell me you forgot to pick up wine? I spend the afternoon at the hospital with a woman who's got a couple of broken ribs, whose husband still has the kids. This is so messed up."

"What?"

"Nothing. Jesus. Get with the program." Her fists hang clenched at her sides.

He reaches to hold them. "Come here."

"What's wrong with you?" She yanks her hands away.

"I'll just be a minute." He picks up the steaks and turns for the door.

"I'm pregnant."

He stares at the blood seeping from the meat and sets down the plate. "What? How?"

"Wrong thing to say."

"Sorry. I'm just a little surprised."

"You don't sound happy."

He knows this voice of hers too well, the defiance and disdain in it. He tries to remember the last time they slept together. A few months ago after one of their fights. She'd discovered the newspaper with his check marks beside bachelor suite rentals. She'd been deep into the wine and came into the guest room, slid in next to him naked except for a pair of cowboy boots. She pinched the folds on his stomach, slurred, "Let's start a family." She got on her knees and faced the wall in the dark, her palms flat against it, and told him to ride her, cowboy. He pressed himself into her and began to stroke, the slap of his belly mocking him against her bottom. She twisted her head around and told him to give it to her harder. He closed his eyes, imagined she was the young woman he'd seen at the roadside 3 & 93 Dairy Bar, and ground into her, grabbed her boot heels, wheezed and gasped, lost in his own world, oblivious to her beneath him. Dani begged him to slap her and pushed herself back against him so that they lost their rhythm. She leaned her face against the wall, reached behind, dug her hands into the flesh of his buttocks and pulled him into her again. But he couldn't finish. He remembered waiting for daylight to break into the room, listening to her finish herself off next to him.

"You going to say anything?"

He considers challenging her, testing her with questions to get at the truth, but it would only give her an opportunity to take out her frustrations on him. He can't afford another sleepless night in the spare room, his senses heightened and alert, listening for the sound of her moving around in the house.

"That's great news, baby. We have to celebrate." He picks up the plate and heads outside, slaps the steaks onto the grill, and stabs them with a fork on both sides as bursts of flame flash around the raw meat. From the small deck in the backyard, he can make out Dani inside the kitchen, pouring herself a glass of wine, drinking it in several deep gulps before pouring herself another. Lonnie closes the lid, turns the gas on high, and waits for the meat to cook.

V

Lonnie and Ricky sit at the bar, the Six at Six show just ended. Ricky's favourite—six women on stage at the same time, stripping and fondling each other, their breasts like helium-puffed balloons brushing against one another's backs. Lonnie finds it overwhelming, a depressing blur of too many naked bodies. Ricky reads the letter aloud.

Dear Romeo,

I'm a simple woman with simple tastes who's wasting her English degree at a feedlot. Average height, average weight, winning smile, fabulous legs. I'm a closet-geek but I hide this by making fun of people I don't know. I'm divorced but not a home-wrecker. I may or may not go gently into the good night. Short or long term, dating me will be a gamble. I'll leave my toothbrush on your sink after our second date. I'll be a bit of a gamble in the bedroom, too. I'm a little curious about bondage but we can never try it at my house because my ex-husband lives in the basement and will hear us. Oh yeah, I do a bit of stand-up comedy, so likely our relationship will end up in a joke. Still interested?

"That's one crazy woman." Ricky dumps the letter on the table, fixes his eyes on the empty stage.

Lonnie folds the letter and puts it in his pocket. The stripper talks to the DJ, hands him a cassette tape. She holds a glass of soda water, a red straw poking out. Lonnie is struck by how she has transformed herself from the woman at the laundromat. "She sounds honest. Upfront. No bullshit."

"She sounds like a cow."

Lonnie pulls the letter out of his pocket, re-reads it, searches for hidden meaning. He feels foolish for sharing the letter with Ricky, slips it back in his pocket. The stripper laughs with the DJ.

"I'm just messing with you." Ricky puts his arm around Lonnie's shoulder and squeezes him close, smacks him on the back. "Seriously, she sounds like a live one. You might have lucked out."

Lonnie studies Ricky's face for mockery.

"I'm not kidding." Ricky nods toward the stage. "You should check her out. A guy like you needs a beer and a piece of tail to keep his sanity."

The DJ cuts the canned music, taps his microphone. "Gentlemen, what you've all been waiting for, all the way from our own little valley down the road, you might call her your neighbour, if you're lucky, let's put your hands together and show some love for Ms Shelby Sweet." Men whistle and clank their beer bottles against the tabletops. Lonnie turns. Shelby prances to "You Shook Me All Night Long."

Schoolgirl theme. Tartan skirt, white dress shirt unbuttoned, tied in a knot at her navel, pink bra, red tie. Horn-rimmed glasses, her blonde hair tied up beneath a black beret. She glides around the stage, swings a stack of books tied together with twine. She sets them down and picks up a long ruler, strides along the stage-side seats, knocks ball caps off men. At a table of balding insurance brokers, she points to a red-faced man with thick jowls, slides her fingers along the ruler, holds up her thumb and index finger a couple of inches apart and pouts. The men laugh and clink their highball glasses together; their eyes glisten at the shared joke. Shelby spins away and points to Lonnie, squats down in front of him, lifts her skirt to expose pink lace panties. She slides her hand in front of the silk panel and taps it with her palm. He stares, silent, unblinking. She pulls his head forward and slips the skirt over him. She smells fragrant, like candy floss. He closes his eyes and feels a heat, a growing tension in his groin that pushes fiercely against the denim of his jeans. He shifts, relieved he's got the cover of the table. She pushes him away, smacks the back of his wrist with her ruler. He yanks his hand back.

Ricky laughs. "Jesus Christ, if you don't tie the blocks to her, I will."

Lonnie locks in the scent of her, the softness of her inner thighs, the gleam of her anklet.

Shelby unties her shirt when the song ends, slips it off her shoulders. Lonnie stares at the silver key around her neck as the next song plays, the damp skin at the base of her throat pulses. He memorizes her act, tries to fit her into his mind, his life, so that by the time she shakes out the blanket, crawls toward him on her hands and knees, the key dangling and swinging back and forth between her breasts, spins onto her back, and smiles at him through legs spread apart high in the air, he's decided that she's his girl.

After the music finishes, she sits up and saunters around the stage, takes her time to bend and pick up the tips scattered around. Crumpled five- and ten-dollar notes. Some folded in half, one folded in the shape of an airplane. "Christ." Ricky shakes his head. "Makes you wish you were a young buck, huh?"

"I better get a move on."

"You cooking dinner again?" Ricky laughs. "Go on. Get out of here. Don't keep her waiting."

"We still on for tomorrow?"

"Only if you get a day pass from the warden."

When Lonnie gets home, Johnson's youngest son is pushing his dump truck around the yard. The dog wags his tail and barks. Johnson's wife rushes out of the house; her face is pale, her eyes red as if she's been crying. The boy throws a fistful of dirt at her legs. She picks him up by the armpits, nudges him toward the house where Johnson yells from inside. The dog cowers, wags its tail slowly. She strokes its face and ears and it licks her hand. She smiles, continues to pet it. Johnson yells again.

Lonnie nods to her before he goes inside and closes the door. Although it's not late, Dani has turned off the lights. She will grill him about his whereabouts, and he'll make up a story. She'll be too tired to argue, and they'll sleep in their separate rooms, their lies like a wedge jammed between them throughout the night.

VI

The next day Lonnie and Ricky lay on top of a rise in the Flathead Valley that affords them a view of a meadow crowded with bursts of bright wildflowers. Behind it, a bench of striated rock.

"Just as wild as when the Kootenai wandered through here," Lonnie says.

"Enjoy it while it lasts, big man. They're going to start ripping the top off that mountain over there, create an open-pit mine. Word is, they're going to start developing sections, too. Like at home. Buy stock in coal, my friend. Coal is the future."

"It don't make any sense."

"You've hauled timber from the other side of that ridge. Didn't hear you complaining then." Ricky peers through the scope, glassing the tree line.

"The rocks are over a billion years old. The trees ain't."

"Aren't you full of folklore and facts."

"Going to make a mess of it all." Lonnie picks at the moss on the ground, glances across the valley. "You ever going to get married, settle down?"

Ricky sets the scope down. "Now why in the hell would you ask me a thing like that?"

"Just making conversation."

Ricky picks up the scope and glasses the tree line where it dog-legs to the right. "Easier said than done."

"I need to tell you something."

"Hang on a sec." Ricky lays still. "Jesus." He hands Lonnie the scope.

The buck nibbles on the grass, his muscles ripple with each step. Lonnie counts seven tips on the antlers.

"It's yours, big man."

Lonnie raises his rifle, adjusts the scope, and waits for a clean shot on his neck, just behind the shoulder. The buck is going about his life, simply grazing, unaware that these are his last moments. The thought depresses Lonnie.

"Easy pickings." Ricky stares straight ahead.

Lonnie squints into the scope, his finger against the trigger. He tries to breathe, waits for his pulse to slow.

"Christ, hit him."

Lonnie lowers the gun, shakes his head.

"Since when did you become such a chickenshit?"

"I can't."

The buck darts into the woods.

Ricky groans and shakes his head. "You're fucking weak."

Lonnie winces. "Sorry, bud. Next time. I promise."

"I'm not your wife."

VII

Lonnie drops a stick of wood on the fire and fans it to life. The flames curl in the breeze, the wood burns orange and blue. Ricky has been quiet since they saw the deer, grunts now and then.

Lonnie offers him a beer, which he waves off. Lonnie warms his hands, takes a pull from a bottle of Wild Turkey, and pokes at the embers as he clears his throat.

"Sorry, man," Lonnie says.

"Let it go already. It happens."

"Has it happened to you?"

"No. We're different."

"How so?"

"I didn't marry."

Lonnie looks at his friend, but Ricky stares at the fire.

"And I mean that as a compliment, so don't go twisting it into something otherwise."

"All right."

"You got someone, at least. She may not be perfect, but she's someone to look after." He pokes the fire.

"She's not the woman I married."

"They never are."

"I can't do right by her. I'm pretty sure she finds me revolting." He wants to tell Ricky what she's really like, but Lonnie is afraid he'll laugh at him, think he's joking.

"So what are you going to do about it? Run to another chick you meet in the personals? I'm sure that's gonna work a whole lot better once the sex dies down."

"What's gnawing at you? You've been in a crap mood all day."

Ricky spits into the fire. "I'm tired of getting old before I'm supposed to get old."

"What the hell are you talking about?"

"All this. The peelers. Hunting. Work. Getting pissed. Just a bunch of short trips that lead nowhere. What about the long haul? The epic trip. Terribly flawed but awesome, the ups and downs, the road forking here and there, which fork to take, which to leave behind, never knowing if you made the right choice but always wondering if you did and that wonder hanging like a faint shadow over your life until you make peace with it. Hell, I don't know. I know jack-shit. Maybe I'm having an early mid-life crisis. My point is, I've got no one to take care of me when I'm old. I've got no home. Jesus, it makes me old just thinking about it."

Lonnie laughs. "You're drunk." The fire crackles; Lonnie rubs his hands over the flame. "Have another."

Ricky gulps down the rest of the bourbon. "You just don't get it, do you? Why watch the peelers with me when you've got a wife at home? I'm still alone, big man. I stay and watch the peelers by myself long after you're gone, go home alone, eat alone." Ricky's voice is sad in a way Lonnie hasn't heard before. Ricky kicks a log. "What's your excuse?"

Lonnie sips his beer. "The long haul isn't all it's built up to be."

"How do you know? You aren't even there yet. Hell, you're looking to cut it short and abandon ship."

Lonnie tips back his beer, gulps it down, and reaches for another in the cooler behind him. He presses the can against his neck, feels his pulse throb against the coolness of the can. He pries it open, fills his mouth, and swallows. "Yeah, well, I'm on my way and I don't like where we're headed. Maybe it's time to try another route."

"I hear that. Fair enough." Ricky rummages through his pack and pulls out his Smith & Wesson. He turns the pistol around in his palm, the short black barrel dull in the firelight, smooth stock, polished wood finish. He sets it next to himself. "Beer me."

They clink cans and guzzle. Ricky crushes the empty can against the log. He picks up the gun, sticks the barrel in his mouth, unlocks the safety with a click. His eyes are wide open, calm; his index finger steady against the trigger.

"Jesus Christ, Ricky, quit screwing around." A log pops and fizzles in the fire. Lonnie jumps. "Put it down. No more jokes."

Ricky winks and presses the trigger. The gun clicks, its hollowness fills the air. He smiles, dark with regret. He takes the gun out of his mouth, wipes the barrel on his sleeve.

"'Least I've got the balls to pull the trigger." He lifts the pistol, trains it on a tree a few yards away, and shoots. The gun booms out and kicks back Ricky's arm, startling them both. A dull, sucking thud in the tree, the echo of the gun blast reverberates across the valley.

Lonnie lunges at Ricky and snatches the gun. He grabs Ricky beneath the jaw and squeezes on his throat. "That was a sick fucking joke."

Ricky's hand shakes until he lets go. "Didn't think it was loaded. Christ."

Lonnie empties the clip in his palm, the casings cool against his skin, and slips them in his pocket.

Ricky laughs. "I don't know what's wrong with me."

"It's not funny. I should take it out of your hide. Jesus."

"It's not in you to fight back."

Lonnie tosses the gun at Ricky and reaches for another beer, slams the cooler shut, squeezes the beer can. He wants to pulverize it, feel the metal rip in his palm, the hot ooze of blood run off his elbow. He can't tell Ricky how each night he wakes up in the guest room bed, drenched in sweat, certain that he's heard a kitchen drawer open, Dani lurking in the dark. That he sits up, his hand under the bed frame, gripping the baseball bat, his ears and skin electric, listening for the slightest creak before he can ease back down and lie awake until his alarm clock rings, startling him just the same. He hands the can to Ricky. "You gave me one helluva scare. Long haul, my ass."

VIII

A few days later, when Lonnie's supposed to meet Dani and friends for a drink to celebrate her pregnancy, he parks his rig behind Robin's Donuts, changes into clean clothes in the front seat. He knows it's a lie; he's seen the opened boxes of tampons, the wrappers tossed in the bathroom garbage basket, but he knows Dani will carry on the deceit for as long as she can. The donut shop is empty, canned music plays overhead. He washes his face, shaves, and wets his hair in the washroom. Satisfied with the way he looks, Lonnie sits down in a booth, taps a teaspoon on the tabletop. Two teenage girls with bad acne gossip behind the counter. A Native woman wearing a hairnet comes out of the kitchen with a load of fresh honey-glazed doughnuts. The door jangles open and a tall, brown-haired woman enters, looks around, notices Lonnie's over-sized beige shirt, smiles. He stands, shakes her hand.

"You must be Romeo." She laughs. "My friends call me Karen." Her grip is firm. She looks him in the eye before glancing over him.

"Lonnie. Can I buy you a coffee?"

"Tea. Please."

At the counter, one girl hands him a pot of tea; the other takes his money. Lonnie feels their eyes on him; their razor-quick teenage judgments ridiculing him. They look past him at Karen.

He slides the teapot across the table. She wears a fleece vest and tight jeans. Angular face, nice teeth. He admires her thin wrists, long fingers, short nails. No makeup. He's grateful that the table hides the folds in his stomach. "Well, isn't this awkward."

She lifts the lid, moves the teabag back and forth, snaps the lid closed, pours a cup. "What do you want to know? Ask anything."

"I've never done this before. It feels strange."

"Listen, honey, who are we kidding? It is strange." She laughs. "I'll start then. What happened to your eye?"

He's silent.

"You a fighting man? I don't mind tough guys. Really. Come on, give me all the gory details. Did you kick his ass?"

He leans back. "What made you reply to my letter?"

"I liked the humour in it. You wouldn't believe the things guys say. Your letter was refreshing. Sweet, naïve." She sips her tea. "You really put yourself out there, you know? Are you looking for a one-off type of thing? Because if you are, that might be okay. We'll have to wait and see."

Her directness startles him, makes him feel uneasy. Yet he knows if he tells her about Dani, she'll suspect he's lying; a tactic to win her over. Or she'll be speechless, think him a coward. He sits up and clears his throat. "I drive a logging truck and live over in Bull Head. My wife's a social worker, but don't let that fool you. She says she's pregnant, but it's a lie to keep me around because she knows I want to leave her. I like playing pool and hunting. My only friend is a guy named Ricky, but he almost whacked himself playing a prank the other night." Speaking plain and honest invigorates him.

"And your eye?"

"My wife has let herself go. She doesn't give a damn anymore."

"What does that have to do with your eye?"

"That's personal."

Karen shakes her head. "Personal, huh?" She fidgets with the teabag label, looks around the donut shop, glances at her watch.

He stares into his cup and lets out a long sigh. "Fuck it. She did it." His face burns with humiliation.

"Your wife?"

He looks down, nods with resignation.

"I don't know what to say. I'm sorry to hear that. Is she okay?"

He raises his head, narrows his eyes. His jaw tightens. "I've never raised a hand against her."

"That's not what I meant."

"What did you mean?"

She touches his wrist. "I just meant, why? How? Was she provoked?"

He squeezes his jaw with his hand. "If I knew the answer to that, I wouldn't be here, would I?"

She stares at him and shakes her head. "That's a helluva introduction. Seriously. I appreciate you telling me, but what's next? What's going to top this? 'Cause sure as sunshine, when guys tell you something right off the bat, there's always something bigger looming."

"Not one for sympathy, are you?"

"Honey, I can handle a lot in a man, but not one who's angry or pissed off at the world. I can't compete with that. You write a helluva letter, though, I'll give you that." She stands and offers Lonnie her hand. "Nothing personal, all right?"

They shake hands and she walks out, past the snickering girls. He waits until she drives away before he gets up, climbs into his truck, changes into his work clothes, and drives home.

Dani has left a note on the kitchen counter next to an empty wine bottle and glass. *Northerner. Sally and Grant. To celebrate. Remember?*

Lonnie glances at the clock above the fridge. A little past ten. He turns the note over and writes: *Sorry. Long day. Got home late. Steak at the Old Elevator tomorrow?* After he re-reads it, he crumples it up and tosses it in the garbage.

He flicks off the lights, climbs the stairs, takes a hot shower, and lies down on the guest room bed. He sets the alarm for four a.m. and stares at the ceiling, plays the conversation over, the way Karen's smile mocked him, the girls giggling behind the counter, the shock on her face when he told her about Dani. What the hell does she know? He wonders what Shelby does after work, what her life is like, where she lives in town. He's surprised that he feels fortunate to have Dani rather than have to be out there, meeting the Karens of the world. Safer, more secure, despite the baggage that comes with it. He replays each movement of Shelby's body when she slipped off her clothes, tugs himself half-heartedly before turning on his stomach and falling asleep.

Lonnie wakes to a blunt, solid pain that slams the wind out of him. He gasps and coughs, surprised by another blow to the stomach. He's disoriented, blind in the dark, the taste in his mouth metallic like aluminum. A fist cuffs the side of his head, rings in his ears; sounds are muffled, vague, and dull. He reaches for the nightlight, but he's kicked in the side by the hard point of a shoe and cries out.

"You fat bastard. Why do you always fuck up and embarrass me in front of our friends?"

Lonnie turns to see if Dani's holding something, but can't tell in the dark.

"Don't you dare move." She kicks him again, hits a rib, the pain slices sharp. Bile rushes into his mouth.

"Stop." His voice bubbles out of him like a strange animal moaning. He curls up, tucks his head into his chest.

The heel of her hand smacks his ear. Her knees dig into his back and choke the breath from him. "Where were you tonight? Where were you?"

"Working."

"Bullshit." She drives a fist into his ribs. "Where were you?"

His eyes sting and he tries to catch his breath, gulps air in half-panicked wheezes. "Settle down. You're wasted. I can't talk to you when you're like this."

"Then fight back." She slaps him again on the skull. "Hello, anyone home? Nope, nothing going on in there. Even if you managed to pay some stripper to fuck you, you still couldn't please her."

He waits, tense, his back turned to her, feels around beneath the bed for the bat. His fingers close tightly around the wood. He sits up, the bat clenched in his right hand.

She holds the crumpled letter from the dashboard of his truck. "Personal ads? Seriously? You couldn't remember to at least get rid of them? You're pathetic." She begins to cry. "You've wasted my best years. Greatest mistake of my life, marrying you. I hate myself for what you've turned me into."

She sobs on the edge of the bed, her shoulders shaking. He lets go of the bat and rolls it beneath the bed. He considers touching her, laying his palm on her back to help comfort her, but he knows this might provoke her further. She lies down away from him, curled into herself like an infant, and soon begins to breathe deeply.

He watches her sleep. She looks the same as when he first met her, sweet and youthful, in the bloom of her life. He gets out of bed. Pain knifes through his body as he dresses. He goes outside, smells cigarette smoke, and sees a red ember in the yard at the Johnson's. The dog barks and he hears Johnson say, "Sshhh." Lonnie climbs into his truck, locks the door, and leans against it. He balls up his jacket, rests his head against the window, and waits for morning to come.

IX

After he hauls his last load the next day, Lonnie parks behind the bar. He fixes his hair in the rearview to hide the bruise on his forehead, changes his clothes in the front seat, and enters through the back door.

He sits down where he can watch the NO ENTRY door and waits for the next show, flashes a hundred-dollar bill to the waitress. "Bring me a high-test every ten minutes until I run out of money." He peels off a twenty, hands it to her. "Your tip." She raises her eyebrows, stuffs both bills into her cleavage.

A dancer hangs plastic beer jugs off her breasts, jiggles them against each other; the next dancer contorts herself in strange configurations on the pole. A third dancer tears tiny holes in her tip money and pulls the bills over her nipples. Lonnie drinks his beer fast and asks the waitress when Shelby Sweet is scheduled. The waitress leaves him another beer, shrugs her shoulders. He hands her the empty bottle.

The No Entry door opens, Shelby steps out, and Ricky follows, a stunned look plastered on his face. She holds his hand and they pause at the DJ booth. Ricky lights her cigarette, then his own. He leans toward her ear; she smiles. Ricky glances over at Lonnie, points a finger at him, and shoots, laughs. Lonnie guzzles his beer and stumbles out the back door.

At the edge of the parking lot a small doe feeds quietly on the brush. Lonnie lurches toward his truck, climbs up inside, and sits, slamming his head against the steering wheel. "You dumb-ass, stupid fat fuck."

He digs for his keys in his jeans, pushes the right one into the ignition, waits for the red lamp to glow. He strikes his head again, touches the wound on his forehead, sees blood on his fingertips. The doe lifts her head to look around and leans down to continue feeding. Lonnie watches her for a while, feels for the rifle behind the seat, slides out of the cab.

He staggers, uses door handles of pickups and sedans for balance, stops at a Chevy where he leans his elbows on the front hood, squints down the barrel at the doe's brown neck. His heart hammers and he can't breathe. He waits and takes a deep breath, exhales slow and easy, and pulls the trigger. The blast booms out and echoes across the parking lot; the kickback smashes into his shoulder like a punch and sobers him. The doe's head whips down as if yanked from below, and then it staggers to its knees, confused, before keeling over on its side.

A faint, sugary taste of cordite hangs in the air. Lonnie walks toward where the doe thrashes, her head snatching back and forth. Pine needles and dirt collect in dark wet clumps on her neck. Her eyes roll with panic. From the bar, the DJ's muffled voice announces Shelby Sweet. The shouts of men, the slam of a door. Lonnie sucks in a mouthful of cold air, exhales, and spits. The deer convulses, braces herself. He touches her forehead. She twitches furiously against his hand. He tries to comfort her, stroking her head as she flails.

Lonnie stands, reloads, and sights in. The hairs on the doe's neck are white-tipped, the bullet hole floods red against the soft white and brown of her hide. His finger rests on the trigger, his breath calm and measured.

"Go on now," he whispers. "Go on home."

FENCES

MAURICE LAY IN his tattered sleeping bag, peered around the one-room cabin in the pre-dawn glow. A yellowed calendar, thirty-five years old, hung on a steel spike next to faded pink stubs from raffle tickets bought for the valley's Rodeo Queen contest. A stack of his wrinkled and warped hunting magazines sat beneath a rack that held two well-polished rifles; a washcloth, dishtowel, flannel shirt, and navy work pants drooped from a clothesline hanging near the woodstove. A worn Bible jammed with various bookmarks—an obituary of their father clipped from the newspaper, blades of grass, and turned-over page corners—rested on a small table next to him.

He glanced to where his brother Harold was snoring, burrowed deeper into his bag, and drew it over his head to cover his ears. The snores rattled through the room, caught deep in Harold's throat before they whistled out. Maurice slipped out of bed, pulled on his overalls, the binder twine in loops over the bulk of his flannel shirt and wool sweater. The floorboards creaked beneath his boots. He examined the door. Still too drafty. Needed more deer hair and moss to chink the cracks. He pushed open the door and closed it quietly behind him, stopped the shrivelled beaver's tail from swinging back and forth, scratching the wood like a coarse pendulum.

The magpies were edgy, but it was too dark for them to move from the cottonwoods. Here and there, a nervous peep. An iron-grey sky in the east where the stars were dulling. A coyote loped in the distance, glanced over its shoulder, cut south across the summer pasture. About an hour 'til sun-up. Chilled air crawled down from Bull Head Mountain, chased Coal Creek, rose out of the coulee, and flowed over the stubbled bunch grass. Starlight and sagebrush on his tongue. He could taste winter coming on.

His horse cropped grass; mist streamed from her nose as she tossed her tail. She was sooty black with a silver mane. A good find some years ago, an auction horse, his favourite, strong working stock that never quit or let him down. A magpie sat on her back; the muscles on her withers stuttered under its feet like tightly coiled ropes.

Lately, she didn't move right. The bump on her foreleg, just below the knee, had grown larger. She shifted her weight from left to right. He knew she would rest a while longer, wait for the stars to fade as the sun rose. She blinked at him, eyes like gems. A narrow white stripe on her nose. Not a smart horse, nor a great horse. Just a horse that got the job done. She needed a rest and a good fattening before the winter.

He walked past her, past the Delco generator, toward the pickup truck.

■

Fred ran a tavern in town and had personally delivered the used truck and generator a few days ago. Maurice and Harold had gone to high school with Fred's father, Orin, but dropped out to work the ranch after their own father died. The brothers knew their ideas didn't cotton with town. That was over sixty-five years ago. Now that Maurice and Harold were on the downward slope tumbling toward eighty, Fred kept a promise to his father to update them on their business transactions, but really, Maurice knew he welcomed any excuse to check up on them.

"She's a beauty." Fred kicked his truck door shut. "And she's all yours."

Fred handed Maurice a bank draft for $67,500.47 and a bag of Oreo cookies to celebrate their latest run at the cattle auction.

Maurice turned away, took a deep breath, and examined the cheque carefully. He held it up in the sunlight, squinting before he stuffed it in his overalls and gave his brother the cookies. Harold tore open the package, split one in half, and scraped the cream off each piece with his front teeth. Maurice shuddered at the sound and eyed the truck. Neither of them had driven a vehicle other than their tractor. Their ranch was blessed with streams and wooded groves and some of the valley's best grass for livestock; horses got them everywhere they needed to go.

"Best if you take her back with you." Harold's teeth were blackened with bits of cookie. "If it's got tits or wheels, she'll give us trouble. No use for her here."

Maurice booted the ground, stole peeks at himself in the reflection from the truck's window. White wisps of hair poked out from beneath his baseball cap, faded brown with stitching across the front that read *Never Trust a Man Who Doesn't Drink*, an ironic gift from Fred since Maurice never touched the stuff. Now that they had a generator, costs would shoot up. No telling how high if they used the truck. It didn't feel right. Little leaks sink great ships—that was Harold's philosophy.

"What do you say, Maurice?" Fred said. "Give that horse of yours a rest. Test it for a few weeks, see how it works for you."

Maurice took a deep breath of the cool air coming down off the mountain. He felt Harold's eyes survey him and nodded to Fred. Harold shook his head.

"Did you want me to deposit that cheque, or are you aiming to hold onto it for a rainy day?" Fred laughed.

Maurice pulled the money from his overalls and handed it to Fred. He stood silently with Harold as they watched Fred's truck recede on the dirt road in the distance, a trail of dust behind him.

■

Maurice glanced toward the cabin. Harold wouldn't be awake for another hour, when Maurice got the stove fired up. His heart pounded in his chest, echoed in his ears. He slid his fingertip along the weathered paint on the truck's hood. Shivers shot through his arms. He grew bolder and ran his palm along the cold metal, traced the words with his calloused fingers: H-A-R-V-E-S-T-E-R, in large letters; *International*, like handwriting. He steered his hand along the curve of the wheel well that was gently sloped toward the headlights, grazed the silver circles that surrounded them clockwise and then counterclockwise, and stroked the metal grill quickly across the slats, strumming a steel song before he climbed inside and closed the door. Fred had left the keys in the ignition, but Maurice didn't touch them. He checked the rearview. Dissolved starlight. Beaver tail still. Pewter bowl sky. He took off his ball cap, licked his fingers, slicked back his hair, tucked a few strands behind his ears before he put his hat back on. A bit late to worry about appearances.

Maurice held the steering wheel and leaned back. Beyond the dashboard, Bull Head Mountain soared. He squirmed himself comfortable and turned the radio dial, dropped his right hand to his thigh. That didn't feel right, so he gripped the steering wheel with both hands and then dropped his left hand to his thigh. That didn't feel right either. He turned the window lever, lowered the window, and propped his left arm up. A breeze blew in, filled the truck with a brisk flush of damp air. His horse snorted; the cabin door opened. Maurice rolled up the window, slipped out of the truck, snapped the door closed, and hurried to his horse.

Harold stood in front of the cabin. "You're awake awful early."

"Couldn't sleep." Maurice stroked his horse's leg.

"You forgot to make a fire. Again."

Maurice looked up. Harold had a stare that could drop a grizzly.

Harold nodded toward the truck. "She's a goddamn eyesore."

"I guess so."

"You guess so, do you?"

Maurice felt Harold's gaze burn into him. He looked down at his own boots and was confused to see that he was wearing one gumboot and one work boot.

"Fifty-percent chance of rain today, eh... boss?"

Maurice flinched at the way Harold paused before he called him boss, the tone he used when he tried to get Maurice to talk.

"Don't you be getting crazy on me, old man."

"I'm sane as they come. We both know that."

"Do we?" Harold chuckled. "You're so wound up, couldn't pull a pin out of your ass with that tractor."

"Maybe you should talk less and get that generator fired up. I'm needing some coffee."

"Damn thing makes a racket. Costs too much to run. Maybe you should just fix us a fire so I can brew the coffee."

"I'll get right on that, boss." Maurice tipped his hat to his brother.

■

The brothers saddled their horses and crossed the trampled grass where their stock had fed during the summer. They climbed a rocky hummock and descended to the tall grass of the winter range. There were several sections of fence to run, and time was tight before the wind would carry snow down the mountain and blanket the landscape. They dug out the ground with sharp picks and used the blunt backs of axes to pound fence posts into the chunky, unforgiving ground. Both brothers tested each post with a firm shake and piled up rocks and dirt at the base before they moved on to the next. Harold slathered roofing tar on top of the exposed end of the post, a trick he learned from their father, to waterproof the ends. Once the fence posts were set, they strung barbed wire from post to post and stretched the wire with an old clamp they had used for years, hooked the end to a come-along, and pushed open the jaws. Maurice laid the wire in the open groove, and Harold pulled on the hook to close the mouth of it, ratcheting the come-along until the wire was tight. Occasionally he let out a low chuckle, as though in conversation. Maurice looked up to see what he laughed at, but Harold's eyes never strayed from the wire.

By late morning, their wrists were sore and the sun was high and cold, so they broke for coffee. They held the cups close to their faces; the dry tufts of grass whispered all about them. Harold squatted and picked up a sun-bleached horse skull in the sagebrush. He held it in front of his face and whinnied at Maurice. "Help, I'm dying."

"You keep horsing around like that and we won't get any work done." Maurice pulled the skull away from Harold.

"Where's your sense of humour gone to, boss? 'Member that hired hand we had last year? You put a dead mouse between two slices of bread. Had a sense of humour then."

Maurice contemplated the skull, turned it in his hands. Frail and brittle. Rows of tombstone teeth, loose and rattling in their plots. Dirt trickled out of the empty eyes. He loved in horses what he loved in the land, muscular and flawed, graceful yet brutal. The grass thrashed softly. The hired hand didn't trust the brothers after the mouse sandwich. Maurice and Harold had warned him about the electrified fence meant to ward off bears, but he threw himself at it to see if it worked. Maurice found the man on his knees beside the fence grabbing his head with both hands, complaining of a headache.

"That hired hand weren't right, and your horse's knee ain't right," Harold said. "The lump is growing bigger."

"I heard you the first time." Maurice set the skull down in the grass.

■

In the cabin, under the harsh glow of a bare light bulb, Maurice flipped through a tattered copy of *Mule Deer*. Harold braided rawhide, hummed to himself, stopped and started the same indecipherable tune in the same place, as though he couldn't remember the next note, as though he were doing it intentionally. The generator groaned against a moonless sky, the windowpane rattled. Maurice tossed the magazine on the dirt floor, put on his cap.

"Where you headed, boss?"

"Checking the horses. Worked them hard today."

"We just fed them an hour ago."

Maurice grunted and turned toward the door.

"You mean your horse?" Harold lifted his head from the strands of rawhide he weaved.

Maurice faced him. "She's got three strong legs. She'll be fine."

"Make yourself useful. Turn off that racket when you come back in. Damn thing whines like a dog in heat."

A cold wind scrubbed the dark night clear. Stars flickered dimly like small tears in the vast black fabric of the world above. Maurice strode past his horse toward the truck, opened the cab door, and climbed in. He jumped back, startled. The horse skull stared at him from the passenger seat. He shook his head and let out a low chuckle. Stark light slanted out of the cabin's window behind him. The generator clattered on. He touched the pedals with his gumboot. First the gas, then the brake. Then he pushed in the clutch, released it, held the gearshift on the steering column. Opened and closed the glove box. Slid open the ashtray. Empty. Pushed it back in. He leaned back against the seat and shut his eyes, tried to piece together the dream from the previous night, the same dream he'd been having since Fred stopped by. Something about a field strewn with boulders. His hobbled horse galloped through the tall grass, dodged rocks, her silver mane flowed and flapped like flags. It was always too dark to see in the dreams and everywhere he tried to look, boulders closed in around him. When his eyes adjusted to the light, he saw that the boulders had turned into trucks, their menacing grills growling as they bore down on him. He had awoken himself shouting after his horse as she ran and faded in the distance. Across the room, Harold was staring at him.

Maurice got out of the truck, trudged to the generator, and turned it off. His ears still buzzed as he caressed his horse's razorous flanks. Her bump felt hot and knobby. He resisted the urge to squeeze it, petted her neck and shoulder until her breath settled into a slow rhythm.

■

For the next three weeks the brothers fenced the winter range with quiet resolve, a seasonal race against the inevitability of winter. Wind raged across the hardscrabble land, shook clumps of skeletal sagebrush, whipped dirt into malevolent swirls that scuttled upward into black funnels boring into the sky. Fresh snow crawled down the peaks each day, caked the treetops like lime dust. Coyotes slunk beneath the fences the brothers had built, and whitetails hopped over them with ease. The brothers ran fence to keep out neighbouring livestock, to warn away the hobby farms that would inevitably appear as the land around theirs was sold off in small parcels. Harold hummed and chuckled while he worked. Maurice was grateful for the wind, for the way it carried Harold's sounds away from him. His horse had grown thinner and he watched her chew on parched grass, legs quivering, the bump on her foreleg like a clump of briar below the knee.

Maurice limped her back toward the cabin, the faint light from the windows hove into view. After he fed and brushed her, the horse stood with her leg cocked. He sat in the truck for a few minutes, marvelled at the buttons and dials, traced the slope of the dash before heading into the cabin for the night.

■

Both brothers huddled around the stove; the wind rattled the cabin, and when Maurice leaned away from the stove to pick up a magazine, he felt a cold draught on his neck. He pretended to read the magazine, but watched Harold push a small patch of cloth soaked in solvent down the throat of the rifle. Harold removed it, brushed the gun out with a damp copper brush, swabbed out the chamber with tissue paper, held the rifle up in the light, and squinted into the barrel. Maurice knew Harold wouldn't clean out the bolt lug recess, like he would himself. Harold would polish the wooden stock with oil and varnish because he liked to keep it smooth. Maurice turned back to his magazine.

"Head or heart?" Harold pointed the rifle at him.

"Put that thing down. She's old, is all."

"She's no use."

"Put it down." Maurice rolled up the magazine and clenched it.

"Our time is coming soon enough." Harold lowered the gun, hummed to himself in a low drone. He stood and put the rifle on the rack.

"You want me to take you around back when you're of no use?" Maurice said.

"Wouldn't expect anything less."

"Maybe that time is now." Maurice unlatched the stove door

and watched the faint coals pulse. He tossed the magazine on the fire and fanned it to life with his palm. The pages curled and twisted in the draught and burned orange and blue. "Fred should be coming around any day now to pick up the truck and generator. We can go back to living in the dark ages. Happy?"

"I'm getting tired of your talk. It's hurting my ears." Harold's voice rose above the generator. "If you don't do something about that horse, I will."

"You don't know squat about her." Maurice got up to leave.

"I know she's got three legs, and if God meant for horses to have three legs, He wouldn't have given them four. Christ, you've lost your horse sense."

"She's got no quit in her. Maybe she prefers having three legs—ever consider that?" Maurice slammed the door shut. As he walked toward the truck, he heard Harold shouting inside the cabin.

■

Maurice woke with a start and tried to remember his dream, but Harold's breath whistled in a steady stream of snores. He crept out of his sleeping bag, dressed in the dark, pulled down the 12-gauge, and grabbed two boxes of shells. He listened for Harold's next breath, took a step toward him, but stopped when Harold resumed snoring. Maurice shut the door behind him.

The horse shifted her weight and shook her head as Maurice stroked her long velvety nose. He caressed her for a long time, murmured softly, her skin warm and solid against his palm. He ran his hand along her ribs; her flanks poked out, the skin draped off her bones. The tumour below her knee was hard; she snapped her head back when he touched it. He kissed the stripe on her nose. She blinked at him.

Maurice opened the truck door, climbed inside. Sleet blew in from the north. He shook his head and sat for a while, fingers wrapped around the steering wheel, then climbed out and walked back toward the horse. The rifle hung cold and heavy in his hands. She wouldn't make it through the winter. Harold had told him so; Maurice knew it himself. The sleet thickened into swabs like cotton.

The generator loomed dark in the truck bed, drag marks in the dirt partly covered in snow. Maurice tightened his grip on the gun, listened to the swish of his horse's tail. "We're gonna need all the luck there is." He rubbed her nose, swept off the snowflakes. His chest tightened.

Her damp eyes were dark, placid pools of obsidian. He leaned his forehead against her, his eyelashes brushed against the musk of her face, her breath sweet and warm. A magpie squawked and startled him, and his horse jerked her head away. He continued to pet her. She calmed and rested her head in his hand. "This life's hell on all of us."

He heard Harold's voice behind him. "Don't miss."

Maurice turned around. He shifted the 12-gauge in his hand, raised the rifle, and trained it on his brother. Harold took his hands out of his pockets, held them out to the side. Wiry, meager body, clothes loose on him, his hands dangled like two prehistoric clubs pulling down on his lanky arms. Gaunt face, pale and crisscrossed with deep lines, his eyes dull blue. He looked frail, as if the wind would knock the whistle out of him.

"I never miss. You should know that by now."

Harold nodded, his head heavy in the crosshairs. Maurice steadied his finger on the trigger, wiped his eye against his shoulder, and retrained the rifle.

His first shot shattered the windshield; the sound tore open the morning. The second shot blew a hole in the grill. He re-loaded and emptied again into the body of the truck, shooting and re-loading and shooting from different angles. The rifle felt hot and light in his hands. Gaping holes of metal smoked on the truck. Tires hissed until they were flat and useless, the life drained out of them.

"Christ, you gave me one helluva scare." Harold held out his hand, nodded toward the generator. "That one's mine."

Maurice studied his brother and handed him the rifle. "Don't miss."

Harold nodded.

"I'll get the fire started, one stick at a time." Maurice turned toward his horse. She stood on three legs, shifted anxiously, snapped her head back and forth. The creek beds cutting through their property had shrunk beneath a thin sheet of ice, cracked clay along their dried banks, the fields stubbled and coarse. It wasn't her time, not yet, but when it came, it would be ruthless and unforgiving. The gun blasts boomed out behind Maurice as he headed toward their cabin, rough-hewn logs notched and fashioned together, trembling beneath a merciless snowfall.

CUTBLOCK

THEY COME WITH the rest of the treeplanters like a caravan of gypsies borne on a skiff, bobbing on the swells of the inlet across the black chop in an early-morning rain. The boat rocks and pitches on whitecaps as deadheads drift past. They grip the hard wooden benches inside while they play cards and tune their guitars. A lone boy sits outside the cockpit, leans against the gunwale with the woman's dog, tears apart garbage bags to wrap the wet animal that lays at his feet trembling in the cold.

"That boy really likes your dog," her girlfriend says.

"He's just trying to get laid," the woman says.

They pass under lush blankets of forests and chug alongside a sandy beach with a broken dock before coming into sight of a new dock where pickup trucks sit silent in the blue light under a mountainside of Douglas fir. Beyond the trucks, a cutblock, inhospitable save for the gleaming white Quonset near the tree line. The woman sees a man get out of a truck and slam the cab roof with his palm, roll a Drum in one hand, and light it as the boat docks.

They disembark one by one. The woman and her girlfriend hang onto the metal railings, their gumboots slip in the slick.

Water roils through the grates below, a cauldron of something terrible that makes them nauseous.

The man finishes his cigarette and points toward a truck. "That's it, ladies, keep moving, we're in business now. Arm's length. Let's get those boxes unloaded real quick. Stop your whining, it's all in the tree price. Daisy chain." His voice trails off and rises toward the treetops.

The boy stands further down the line and passes waxy tree boxes off the boat, on the dock, up over the metal bridge onto the waiting truck beds. Boxes stamped with *Trees for Tomorrow. Forests for the Future. Keep Cool.* The irony lost on the jaded crew but not on both women who, in the first week of February, had begged their way onto the job and whose limbs now ached like branches burdened with the weight of an early spring snowfall. Trucks loaded, they walk up the road, shovels slung across backs hung with planting bags and knapsacks. Their boots crunch on gravel as if they are marching on brittle bones.

The rain does not let up. Torrents of water cut through the mud around the women's camp, and the tents that have no tarp, like theirs, or are set on low ground, like theirs, are soaked through.

A windstorm slants in rain hard off the inlet, stings their faces. During lulls, orcas swim in pods and follow the crew's skiff to work across the briny waters of the channel from camp. Both women lean into the sleet, plant balsam and fir and yellow cedar seedlings, comfort themselves that at least they'll be in camp soon, dry and warm. But the wind howls, and when they return to the cutblock, the trees and ground glitter with a dusting of sugary snow. The women's tent hangs high in a tree at the edge of the cutblock, flapping like a damp prayer flag, clothes scattered on the forest floor as if they've been hauled out of some great washing bucket, waiting to be pinned up on a clothesline.

"Merry Christmas," the woman laughs, marching toward the Quonset.

Her girlfriend follows, shaking her head. "We didn't know how good we had it before."

"We were living off pogie."

"Yeah, but we were living. This is hell."

"It's snowing in March. What's the big deal? It's not going to last."

"You always think there's greener pastures."

"There are."

Dinner consists of overcooked vegetables and thick tofu slabs drenched in teriyaki sauce to disguise the taste of absolutely nothing. Outside of the Quonset, wind and rain belts the canvas, but the women are dry and after a second cup of cheap brandy, warm. They relax, their worlds open once again after deciding to bolt camp at the end of the shift; they talk about what they will do with their new freedom. Soon the brandy is killed and someone breaks out the beer. They play cards. Someone passes a joint. Someone strums and hums to a guitar. A naked man dances around the woodstove, his dreadlocks swaying in his eyes like thick twigs.

The woman sits close to the boy. He smiles beneath shaggy hair that hangs over his eyes. She keeps her leg against his so she can feel his warmth through her jeans, while her girlfriend sits on the other side of him, drinking faster than the woman has seen her drink before. Another joint makes the rounds. More beer.

The music gets under her skin, spreads through her, loosens her limbs. After another spliff, she finds herself dancing close with her girlfriend, looking over her shoulder at the boy who smiles at them.

"Two more sleeps," her girlfriend says. "And we're out of here. No prisoners."

The woman laughs and breaks away, pulls the boy toward them by his hand, and the three of them dance together, the boy in the middle.

"What's your name?" The woman hears herself giggle. She hears herself ask, "Where you from?" Her girlfriend flings her arms around the woman's neck and kisses her while grinding herself into the boy, but he never replies. He smiles and waits as the three of them dance. The woman kisses her girlfriend deeply over the boy's shoulder. His breath rises and falls in her ear; she kisses her girlfriend again. Her girlfriend pushes the boy away and holds onto the woman, whispers, "Don't do this to me, not after the winter we've had."

The woman hears herself laugh, "You're the one who's wasted."

The girlfriend shakes her head, veers away like a marionette, and throws up in the corner. She slurs, "G'night," and staggers out of the Quonset.

"She all right?" The boy leans on the edge of a table, grinning.

The woman loves the way he moves, like someone at ease with who he is, and she wants to feel that, too. She pulls him toward her, tugs fiercely on the belt loops of his well-worn jeans. They go outside and walk to the edge of the block to the tree line. The storm has broken, and the thin veil of snow is gone, the sky clear and littered with stars like broken glass sparkling on pavement.

The trees dark and tall and fragrant.

"It's as if they're scratching the sky," he says. "No, it's as if they're holding it up."

She tilts her head back and watches the stars, leans into him for balance. "A poet. I should have known."

He smiles. "You ever wonder, what if this is it, what if all you need you have right now instead of thinking that what you need is someone or somewhere or sometime else?"

She feels dizzy looking at the stars and focuses on the trees instead. He's right, they did look like they were holding up the sky. She leans into him again. "For a quiet guy, you sure talk a lot."

■

The woman's tent remains clinging to the branches, high up a tree. She sleeps in the boy's tent with her dog; the boy insists on sleeping on the front seat of his pickup truck, parked nearby. Her girlfriend sleeps alone on a bench in the Quonset. At the end of the shift, as they load the boat for the ride out, the woman tells her girlfriend she wants to stay for another shift.

"He's not the answer," her girlfriend says.

"How do you know?"

"You're just another distraction. Put a dog in the Taj Mahal, and it's still a dog."

"You're jealous."

"He's gonna mess you up. It's all over your face."

The woman stares at herself in the side mirror of the crew truck. Her perpetual grin, strange shiny eyes, pigtails poking out the sides of her toque. "He's different."

"Like hell he is. You'll spend another winter recovering from this one. Why don't you ever listen to me?"

After they disembark from the boat, the girlfriend hitches a ride into town with some of the others from camp. The woman and the boy drive in his truck, speed down the dark highway, pass loaded logging trucks, the yellow centre line unfurling like an umbilical cord on their left. She sits close against the boy, her hand in his thick hair, tugging it. She sees the broken crayons on the dashboard, the dirty handprints on the windows, the toy race car on the floor. And she's sure that if she opens the glove box, she'll see a whole lot more.

For two days in the Reel Inn, the boy and the woman keep the shades drawn, drop ecstasy, drink cheap red wine by the litre, and eat greasy take-out from the Copper River Convenience. Welfare kids run around in the gravel lot, chase each other with water pistols and knock on their door. Fishermen push off in the early dark hours for steelhead.

The boy tells the woman about the home he has built over the years, pouring his planting money back into the house during the off-season. The house now finished, he's bored and needs another project.

He speaks of his partner, how they met in a planting camp four years ago, how she's changed since the birth of his son. His voice softens. "He's a neat little guy. It kills me not to be with him." They didn't have sex anymore, and she didn't look him the eye. Each time he raised the issue, she told him there was nothing wrong, and after a while he decided she wasn't attracted to him, never had been.

"You ever hear of the fatal flaw in a relationship?" he says. "The moment you meet someone you fall for, you get a quick glimpse of the true thing that might drive you apart. You ignore it at the time, you don't even know it to be a flaw, you might even think it's cute or quirky, and you're attracted to it. You even think it's something you can change in them. But it's there, and over time it grows, digging deeper into your life so that one day you stand across a valley from one another with no way of closing the gap because you can't, because you know the thing between you can never be forgotten, it's always been looming there since the beginning." He leans against the headboard, stares at the ceiling. "She hated being alone. I couldn't go anywhere, not even into town to pick up the mail, without her wanting to be with me. At first it was flattering. Like I was important to her and she really loved to spend time with me. But after a while I realized she was just afraid, and it had nothing to do with me."

After the ecstasy wears off, they smoke a joint and drink more wine from the bottle, pass it back and forth, the sheets twisting around them like rope. She spills some on his stomach, the stain spreads across the sheet beside him. She licks his belly and brushes her face against him, looks into his eyes. "So, what's my flaw?"

"You don't have one."

"I'm serious."

"You're too damn pretty." He tickles her fleshy ribs.

"Quit screwing around."

He stops. "Fine. You have trouble following through on things."

"Bloody hell. You don't have to be so harsh."

"Sorry."

"You're the same, anyways."

"No. I'm the opposite. I keep my commitments."

"You mean like the one to your girlfriend?" She knows that she's hurt him because he's silent and turns away.

"Fair enough. Almost all of my commitments."

"Then we should get along just fine, right?"

They laugh, roll in the sheets, smear the wine between them, and when he lifts his face to meet hers, he blurts out the thing she wants to say herself but cannot, should not, will not, not after knowing someone for a few days. She kisses him quickly in reply and turns away, stares at the wall until she falls asleep.

In the morning, on the boat ride back to camp, she sits in the rain with the boy and her dog. "Don't you dare say that to me again unless you mean it, understand?"

The boy says it again, and keeps saying it the rest of the spring. He shouts it across the cutblock when they plant together, murmurs it while they brush their teeth. He tells her in sign language, and he says it with little gifts—an empty wine bottle with wildflowers in it; notes scratched by rock into the waxed cardboard of the tree boxes slipped into her lunch bag. He draws hearts on a sandy beach. Carves them into trees at the edge of the cutblock. He tells her before they go to work in separate crew trucks and again when they get home and share a beer and shower together. Each day he tells her he planted every tree for her. She is surprised by his emotional, theatrical displays of affection, resists it by telling herself that he is infatuated with the idea of his own infatuation. He'll gain his senses and lose interest.

"There's so much beauty in a cutblock," he says one sunny afternoon while they sit on the landing, leaning against flattened tree boxes eating their lunch.

"It's a moonscape. There's nothing here. No birds, no sounds, no trees. Nothing's alive or growing."

"You have to look closer. See the beer can and plastic oil jug with their faded labels? Rusted chainsaw blade. Spray can. Signs of men who worked here for their families. In another month or so, it'll be covered in a sea of pink and green fireweed. After that, snow so deep you won't see the stumps, and it will look like a winter meadow; you'll be able to snowshoe across it. Wouldn't it be great to build a place on one of these, watch the trees you planted grow up around you?"

"It's still a cutblock. Barren and boring."

"It brought us together."

■

In late April, when they are breaking camp, the boy runs over a feral cat that crouches beneath his truck. The cat lifts its head, mouth bloodied and broken, and bolts for cover in the bush; the boy climbs out of the truck and sprints after it. Crew bosses bellow reminders about making the barge in time. The woman runs after the boy, leaps logs, ducks beneath furry branches that scratch and pull at her arms, shouts the boy's name over and over. But it is no use; he's faster and disappears. She gives up, turns around and cautiously walks across the cutblock, over long, grey logs onto springy piles of slash, using stumps as steps, and heads toward the idling trucks.

Her crew boss lays on the horn and shouts, "That's a goddamn dead cat. Let's go." The woman searches the tree line for a sign of them.

Someone shouts. The boy walks out of the bush, cradling the

cat in his arms. He traverses the cutblock with ease and offers the cat to the woman. "I found it where your tent used to be."

She touches the cat's head, inspects its face, and senses it will be okay. In the relief of the moment, of learning something new about the boy, she hugs him ferociously. She starts to cry, and he holds her close, kisses the top of her head.

"It's okay. Everything's okay." He takes the cat from her and holds it up to whoops and hollers from the rest of the crew.

■

The woman begins to depend on him. They spend the rest of the spring together, her dog and his cat between them; she goes to bed early instead of hanging around the campfire late, smoking pot and drinking. She waits a few weeks and breaks the news to him once she resolves she will keep the child. The boy surprises her with his enthusiasm, his tears of joy; he starts a list of names, brings her chamomile tea in the mornings, massages her feet in the evening. He works every day he can, first and last to bag out.

On a rare day off together at the Reel Inn, the boy slips out of bed early and crosses the gravel parking lot beneath a lead-coloured sky. The woman heaves into the toilet, grips the bone-bleached bowl to haul herself up to the window where she wraps a blanket around her bare shoulders and peeks through the filthy curtains. The boy stands hunched over the pay phone, smiling into the receiver before hanging up and returning to the room, the smell of rain clinging to his broad shoulders.

"Did you tell her?" the woman says.

"My son has the flu. She's going through a tough time."

"What about me?" She feels her anger rise, prickling the skin on her neck.

"I'm sorry." He holds her close and gently rocks her. "I'm sorry. You're right." He strokes her stomach and is quiet.

"What's wrong?"

"Nothing. Everything's happening so fast. I need to slow it down."

"What good would that do?"

"Before I came planting, he promised he'd take care of me when I got old." The boy flips the curtain aside and stares out the window. "Christ, he's not even four."

"You can't keep putting this off. It's eating you alive and making us both miserable."

"You don't have to make me feel worse."

"It's not too late to back out."

"I'm not going anywhere."

■

They follow the work, move further north to Meziadin Junction, where the nights are bright as the solstice nears, humming with clouds of black flies and mosquitoes and no-see-ums that crawl through the mesh screen of their tent. When the boy and the woman tumble off to bed after dinner, they kill mosquitoes by flashlight, bloodied streaks and appendages smeared into the blue nylon of their tent walls, until they can sleep in peace, clinging to one another, the cat and dog sleeping against their heads.

The woman begins to dream of trees. Densely packed forests. Trees standing alone on a torn-up landscape of broken branches, stumps upturned on their sides, piles of slash as tall as a house.

Clusters of trees packed along the riverbanks. Tender seedlings in a mound of rich dirt beside a stump. The soft nettles of a yellow cedar, the scent of a jack pine, the sticky sap of a fir.

When the boy tells her she spent part of the night hunched inside the tent, pacing back and forth, screefing the sleeping bag, looking for the perfect place to plant the next tree, she has no recollection of it. She does it again and again; the boy and the cat and the dog sleep against the far side of the tent to give her more space. One night, he stops her and encourages her to lie down, tells her he'll help plant out her trees, takes her shovel and plants a few trees. "See, it's okay, get some sleep." He lays her down and notices blood on the sleeping bag, larger spots than from the mosquitoes they've killed.

They rush through the night along dark and dusty logging roads, thud across the rough corrugated surfaces into corners, speed down the smooth straightaways, rocks pebbling the underside of his truck. Insects smash into their headlights and smack off the windshield. The woman cannot sit so she kneels upright on the seat, rolls down the window, and grips the door to steady herself. She closes her eyes and leans her head out the window, the cold air lashes her, a respite from the cramping that tears at her lower back and insides. The wind obliterates the boy's voice, dust seeps into the cab of the truck; she breathes through her mouth, suffocated with what she knows has gone wrong.

In the emergency ward the boy holds her hand, caresses her forehead, kisses her. "There will be another one." His eyes are filled with tears. "I promise."

She turns away, leans her cheek against the coolness of the wall. "There's nothing keeping you here anymore. Except guilt."

He clings to her more fiercely and weeps. "We'll keep trying. I'll build a house on stilts overlooking a cutblock. We'll raise him and grow old together and watch the forest grow up around us."

"Stop it. You have no idea what you're saying anymore."

∎

During the summer break between contracts, they head south, where the fruit hangs heavy and fragrant in thick orchards and the lake is bathwater warm. They rent a small cabin on the shores of the lake, pre-paying by the week, and settle in.

The boy sets up a wood shop and spends long hours in the outbuilding. When he's not with her in the cabin, the woman misses him or feels lonely, she can't tell which, but she's glad when he returns, filling the cabin with the scent of cedar dust that falls from his arms.

One day the boy takes the woman by the hand and leads her blindfolded to the workshop and unties the bandana. "Look."

A cedar trunk rests on the ground, smooth as morning lake water, the planks merge into one another as one, a whale carved into the wood on top. "It's for you."

"What is it?"

He laughs. "A trunk. Made with scraps from the various cutblocks we've worked on together."

She runs her hands along the smooth wood, traces the contours of the whale's body. "No one has ever made something for me." She kisses him.

"Open it."

The woman lifts the lid. Inside a mood ring sits on the bottom. When she turns around, the boy is bent on one knee.

He slips the ring on her finger. "Will you grow old together with me? I'll get you a proper ring, at home." He holds her hand to look at the ring. "It's turning purple."

"Get up." She takes the ring off and hands it back to him.

He stops smiling and lets out a long exhale. "I know it's not ideal. You deserve better. Much better. And I'll spend the rest of my life seeing that you get nothing but."

The woman covers her face with her hands, turns away, and cries.

"I'm sorry. I promise, I'll head home first thing tomorrow morning, get everything straightened out. Just give me a couple of days."

She turns to face him. "And then what? We'll live happily ever after? Jesus."

He bends over and unties one of his boots, slips it off, and places it in the trunk. "How far can I go with one boot? Keep this as a reminder of what I'm proposing. I need you like these boots need each other."

"I don't want some trite, dramatic, romantic gesture. I want something real."

"Trust me on this."

"Three days? No more sneaking around?"

"Yes."

■

The next morning, he tosses his duffle bag onto the bed of the truck. They hold each other tight in the cool damp air. He climbs inside, starts the ignition, and leans out the window to kiss her.

She will wait one week before loading up her van and driving southeast to Bull Head, the hum of her bald tires a desperate slow song on the blacktop. She won't know where to go once she gets to town, doesn't know the boy's address. So she'll drive around town all day, up and down each street looking for his truck, and sleep in her van at night. She won't know how she'll confront him, but she senses it will be unpleasant; she feels like a fool for imagining a future with him.

After a few days of searching, she'll learn that he took his son fishing, taught him how to read the water and throw a dry fly at the edge of the calm pool, let the eddies move it, wait for the fish to rise along the riffles, and carefully set the hook. She'll learn that he showed his son how to remove a hook and kiss the fish before releasing it back into the river. Perhaps that's what they were talking about before they encountered a black bear and her two cubs on the path. The boy snapped his fishing rod on the charging bear, shouted at his son to run to the truck and wait for him. His son sat crying, huddled in the footwell, clutching his knees, rocking back and forth, waiting for his father to return as darkness fell. She'll learn all this from an article in *The Free Press*, the ink from her fingertips smeared on her face in black streaks.

The woman will agonize about introducing herself to the boy's son and his mother, drive to their house and park nearby, consider what she'll say while his son practices his casts on bright yellow rubber ducks floating in a plastic wading tub in the front yard. She'll see his mother pick him up, hold him like a small sack of feed, and carry him to the porch, smooth out his hair, call out to him when he runs behind the house. She'll see the woman sit on the porch step, lean against the wooden post, and close her eyes against the brightness of the day.

She'll return each day, park out of sight and watch the son and his mother together until one day they leave, drive down the gravel road, the dust settling on the treetops. The door will be unlocked.

The fridge magnets will hold up colourful crayon drawings of a man holding hands with a child in front of a house. A man with a shovel, trees behind him. A cat. Notes for dental appointments long past, a pre-school newsletter, emergency numbers, a reminder to pick up cat litter.

In the bedroom she'll find a picture of the boy on the night-stand showing off a fish on a boat. Countless pictures of his son. Wearing a cowboy hat and holster. A naked toddler on his belly, smiling. Sleeping in a bundle of blankets. She'll open the drawer. A Bible, more photographs, her mood ring tucked away in the back corner. She'll find a picture of the boy, one she took when they were in a fruit orchard, the lake behind him. He smiles back at her, wide and open. She'll pocket the photo, slip on the ring, and close the drawer.

She'll rent a house in town, down the road from the child and his mother. Eventually, she'll inherit family money and buy a tract of logged land on a small rise with a view of the church and cemetery and river. Here, she'll build a modest home. The soil will be rich and black under her nails, stain her fingertips, dark and winey, the smell of lodgepole pine always nearby. She'll give up on trying to scrub it out. Other men will come and go in her life, but embracing them will be like holding charred wood—they will darken her existence with the knowledge that she had once held the one she was meant for.

She will stand on the snow banks along with the other parents and watch the boy's son play hockey, stamp her feet to keep them warm, hear the muffled claps of her gloved hands each time the boy's son makes a good play. She'll genuflect on the hard wooden kneelers and pray for the boy's son at his confirmation, the damp of holy water drying on her forehead. She'll see his mother drop him off at junior high school with a kiss on the cheek, and she'll see the first time he gets drunk at the town dump, the stench of garbage thick in the air as he throws beer bottles and shouts curses from the tailgate of his father's truck at the stout, sluggish bears foraging for trash. She'll follow him as he picks up his date for the high school prom and wait outside the school gym listening to the pounding bass line vibrate off the walls, the early summer evening warm, humming with insects around her. She'll follow them up the mountainside to a turnoff overlooking the valley where the boy's son and his date park, sit on the tailgate beneath the stars, sip beer and laugh before they roll out a blanket on the flatbed for the night. His father's duct-taped fly rod stretched across the gun rack in the rear window.

The woman will slip in through the back of the church and attend the boy's son's wedding, and later, after everyone has left, she'll grab a fistful of confetti and rice from the ground and save it in a small jar that she will keep on the windowsill above her kitchen sink. She'll cut out the birth announcements of each of the young couple's three girls and pin them to her fridge next to the picture of the boy taken in the fruit orchard.

When the son's mother passes away, the woman will attend her funeral, sit in the back of the church, wipe her eyes with a neatly folded handkerchief. In her own final days, the woman will lie in her bed, her head turned toward the window, the sky high and blue, stretched out over the cutblock, held up by the sturdy columns of trees that surround her, each one hand-planted and pruned, watered and thinned, a profligacy of green.

The boy kisses her, and they cling to each other through the window, their foreheads pressed against one another until he kisses her again. The woman lets go of his hands as he slowly eases the truck out of the drive. He honks his horn; the brake lights on his truck wink, then fade in the mist that skims along the skin of the land, rising up into the dazzling morning as he drives away. She waves, knows that in the grand stretch of time, three days is not long to wait and whispers a small prayer, dear God, keep him safe. Across the lake, the outline of the mountains is sharp and serene; up above, the sky shines like a sapphire, blooming brighter as the day opens around her in a warm embrace.

GAS BAR

BECAUSE IT'S THE Thanksgiving weekend, Dwight hangs around with the others at the end of the shift. They are a new crew, green and big-limbed, eager to provide for their families. He doesn't trust them, their tall tales and sloppy work, and by the third beer, he's heard enough. He crushes an empty in his fist, tosses it in the slash, flexes his hand, the knuckles ugly as lug nuts, strands of scars across the top, and shakes out the numbness. He slings the rest of his six-pack, eases into his pickup, and drops the beer in the cooler behind his seat.

In his side-mirror, through the dust, one of the guys throws a can at his truck. Another raises a rifle. When the shot booms out, Dwight lowers his head and glances through the rearview. The men laugh and slap each other's backs, rifle pointed in the air, bottom of a beer can at one guy's mouth. It amazes him that these men have families waiting for them at home. He fishtails out of the turn, flashes his brake lights twice to let them know he's in on the joke, straightens the truck and heads for town.

Dwight punches Merle into the tape deck and "The Running Kind" comes on. The beer buzz hits, and he speeds along a gravel road he knows well. Down the valley, the rain comes fast and blurs a blanket of forest; the clear cuts and fresh slash piles he has helped fell litter the land. Tonight starts another weekend of beer and bourbon and TV, hunkered down in his room, then another five-day shift with the same crew, the same long twelve-hour days—only the trees will change, falling into other cut-blocks and other valleys. Rain smudges the windshield. There's nothing left except for driving and waiting.

Sarah used to love this section. They were going to build a cabin here when the girls got older. Retire. Raise chickens and cultivate vegetables and sip drinks on the porch at the end of the day. The foreman will probably have him cut the valley next spring, and that will be the end of that. He'll take his saw to every one of them and drop them like old friends, the chain chewing their soft bones.

By the time he hits the blacktop, eastward on the Crow, the rain pelts down hard, dimples the dirt shoulder. Others might drive this long stretch with their eyes closed, but not him, not here. He thinks about the holiday weekend feasts Sarah used to put on. The house warm, windows sweating, the girls rushing to meet him at the door in their pink dresses, dragging him to their toy tables with bright plastic cups and saucers. At Twelve Mile he gears down, wipers on high, the rain pounding his rooftop like a sack of thrown marbles. He stops at the big cedar, with the motor idling, gets out, and walks to the tree.

He pulls the black-and-white photo out of his pocket. Sarah's smile is fading, but the girls—Kate, Christine, and little Jody— still have that photo-studio shine as though the picture were just taken. He wipes them with his shirt cuff and stands for a few minutes in front of four small white crosses, a vase of wilted flowers, a brown teddy bear wrapped in plastic. It leaves him feeling useless to think about dinners and work and the oncoming winter—a washed out year. The rain rakes the asphalt, gurgles in the ruts, and spits on the picture. He curls it close to him and says, "See you Tuesday."

He drives slow until he hits the industrial strip on the outskirts of town, pulls into the covered gas bar, parks, and tells the kid to fill it up. A group of miners sit on top of their metal lunch boxes. They smoke, stare down at their boots, wait for the valley's coal corporation bus to pick them up for the graveyard shift. A wet dog lies outside against the garbage can. It cowers when Dwight steps toward it. He bends down and offers the back of his hand. The dog sniffs his fingers cautiously before it, wagging its tail back and forth.

Inside the store, he loads up on pepperoni sticks, a hoagie, and a bottle of Coke, dumps it all on the counter. He reaches for the blue whales. The girls used to squeal over those. He counts out six, two for each, and asks the lady behind the counter for a pack of Export A's.

Outside, a young woman wanders along the service station wall to keep out of the rain. Filthy jeans cling to her skinny legs, her windbreaker soaked through. He shakes his head. She's probably making the rounds out back with truckers whacked out on amphetamines, their families far away; only a matter of time before one of them bangs her up in his truck before dumping her in a ditch on their way home. The glass door rattles as she pushes it open.

Her feet are a mess. Broken toenails, stripped back as though someone had taken pliers to them. "What are you looking at?" she says.

Town unhinges him now, more strange faces, seasonal vagrants coming and going, people who don't give a damn about the place. He nods to her and leaves, closing the door behind him. The miners are gone; he drops a pepperoni stick in front of the dog. Its tail thumps against the garbage can; he stoops down and rubs its ears. It turns on its side, licks his hand. "You're a good dog." He asks the kid who the dog belongs to, but the kid shrugs and turns back to filling up an RV. Dwight thinks about how this dog needs a home and how nice it would be to have some company. He knows this game; he's only fooling himself, so he drops another pepperoni stick and leaves the dog snuffling the ground for more.

He climbs into his truck, slips it into gear, and within minutes the Lamplighter sign comes into view. Good TV and close enough to the house to feel like home, far enough that he won't walk over there when he gets drunk. Cold beer and wine, tavern next door. At the front desk, Alice hands him a fistful of messages. "That realtor isn't one to give up, is he?"

He stuffs the paper in his pocket. "Sorry for the bother."

"Keep pre-paying in advance, and he can call as much as he wants." She returns to her crochet.

He drives around back, buys a fifth of rye and case of beer, slips into his room, peels off his wet clothes, tears the paper wrapper off a stubby glass in the bathroom, pours three thick fingers of rye and splash of Coke. The candy sits in a small white paper bag on the rim of the sink. Goddamn blue whales. He shakes them out onto his palm and squeezes them, but his fingers ache. White knuckle. All the fallers get it. Blue gelatin bleeds on his hand, and he whips them at the bathroom mirror. They bounce off, scatter across the counter, and tumble onto the floor. The inside of the door is scraped in long vertical claw marks, many of them deep, desperate. He touches them, decides someone must have locked up their dog when they went out or something, and slaps the door hard with the flat of his palm. A man who mistreats his dog mistreats his wife. He's seen it time and again with the men he has worked with over the years.

He gets into bed, pulls up the covers, and leans against the headboard, sips slowly. His arms ache like something dead hangs from his shoulders. He lights a cigarette, flicks on the TV. Baseball. Canned laugh tracks. A documentary on elephants. Families move around in herds, led by the oldest female. They swim, run fast, and tear leaves off branches with their trunks. One of the elephants has lost its trunk to a crocodile at the edge of a murky lake and can no longer hunt for food. It makes a rumbling sound in its throat as it wanders the barren country. When the rumbles turn to low-pitched moans, Dwight hits mute. The girls loved every animal they ever met.

He flicks to the adult channel and turns on the volume. Bored sweaty faces, camera angles for circus freaks, a guitar soundtrack that doesn't match the bewildering action. He turns back to the elephant. Every whimper seems to ridicule Dwight until the elephant drops to the ground and lies there, no longer moving. A small procession of elephants gathers around it and stroke the corpse with their trunks. He takes a deep drink, butts out his cigarette, glances at the alarm clock. 6:29 p.m. Already a long night. He pours another, drinks it in a gulp, and thinks of how this room is all the home he has now. The elephant still whines; he hits mute and no longer feels like getting wasted.

He studies the ceiling and waits. 8:03 p.m. TV flashes in the dark room. He gets up and goes to the bathroom. The whales lie on the floor twisted and upside down, and that makes him miserable. He arranges them on the counter side-by-side and feels better after a hot shower and shaving his five-day beard. He dresses, pulls on his ostrich-skin boots, a last Christmas gift from Sarah, and crosses the highway to the Old Elevator.

The restaurant is busy and warm. The young hostess hugs two menus as she greets him. She is too perky when she asks if he needs a table for two. He holds up one finger and remembers that she, too, is someone's daughter. Her neatly plucked eyebrows scrunch as she studies her seating map, drops a menu, and leads him to a table at the back near the salad bar where high chairs line the hallway toward the toilets. She waits until he is seated before handing him a menu and walks away without a word.

He splurges and orders a porterhouse. Couples sit leaning in close across their tables, some with children who maul paper placemats with crayons, others flushed with wine in the candlelight, and he knows what they are thinking—that poor pathetic man, dining alone. He wants to shout how they got it all wrong; he did the best with the time he was given. Now he waits on god knows what. Eating by himself makes him feel mean, gutted, like his chest has been split open and all that's inside is rotting wood. He eats quickly, pays the bill, leaves a generous tip, and walks out.

It's still raining when he crosses the highway and heads toward the Northerner. Beneath the awning, the young woman from the gas bar slouches against the wall, smoking. Her eyes are narrow, and she flashes a grin that unnerves him, one that says, "You can't fool me with those ridiculous boots." He enters the tavern, glad to be amongst the living. Orders a shot of bourbon and a can of Old Style Pilsner. Knocks back the shot, takes a deep sip of beer, motions for another. He turns the can in his hand. The girls used to count the little white bunnies out loud, but he'd turn the can so they'd lose track and have to start all over again. They never tired of that game. He never bought any other beer.

On the small square of parquet floor, a Kootenai woman dances by herself. Eyes bright, her body moves to a beat all its own. He used to watch Sarah dance, guard her from afar. He couldn't believe his good fortune. Fire and gin. Sarah knew how to light him up.

Dwight catches his reflection in the mirror behind the bar. Passes his hand over his eyes and feels too old to be drinking in bars alone. Finishes his beer. The gas bar girl leans against a pillar in the shadows at the back, stares at him. He's had just about all that he can take. He digs in his pockets, pulls out a twenty, and clenches it in his fist. His hands are looser now, thanks to the bourbon, as he makes his way toward the exit.

"Here, take this," he says, handing her the money. She looks at him, and he knows she's sizing him up to see if he's playing her. "Take it."

She's prettier close up, maybe older than he thought, although he can't tell with women.

She doesn't glance at the bill. "You want some company tonight, huh?"

"Nope."

"Nice boots."

He's not sure if she's being sarcastic, asks her name.

"I don't need a drink." Her eyes are glazed and soft, and he thinks she must be high.

"Where's your shoes?"

"Listen, I just need a place for the night."

"I'm not in the mood."

"I just need a room."

"You don't understand. I'm not into it. No offence." He places the money in her palm, but she yanks her hand away.

"I don't need money."

"Everyone needs money."

"That's not true. That's not true at all."

"Suit yourself." He sets the money down on the counter and turns to leave.

"I'm only taking this so someone else don't come along and grab it."

She follows him across the parking lot; her bare feet slap against the wet asphalt. It's nice to have someone next to him, walking. He's wary of her and has nothing to say, but he likes the idea that he could say something and have someone talk back to him.

"Nice weather, if you're a duck," she says.

He can feel her looking at him.

"We might have to build an ark. Though I don't know if we could find two of everything in this hell hole."

"This hell hole happens to be my home."

She smiles and laughs for the first time, and he thinks of how she should be studying at home or helping her mother cook dinner. She slaps his arm. "Ah, yes, of course it is."

He's not sure what she means by that, but she cracks him up.

He holds open the door to his motel room and bows. "Welcome to my hell hole."

Her hair ends are wet and cling to her face and cover her eyes. He hands her a towel, but she ignores it. Offers her a glass of rye. She shakes her head.

"I don't drink."

She opens the night table drawer, pulls out a Gideon Bible, places it on the night stand, flattens her palm on it, closes her eyes, and whispers to herself.

"What's that for?"

Startled, she opens her eyes. "You never know when your card is drawn." She stuffs the Bible in the front pouch of her windbreaker and takes it off, folds it over a chair. "You don't mind if I take this with me, do you?"

She's right, you never know. "Isn't that breaking a commandment?"

The girl hooks the underside of her T-shirt with her fingers, peels it over her head, and tosses it aside. A small gold crucifix hangs from a thin piece of twine against her sternum. "Kill the light."

When it's dark, she finishes undressing silently and climbs into bed. "I've seen it all. C'mon, neither of us are getting any younger."

He kicks off his boots and takes off his clothes, lies on his back next to her with the covers pulled to his chin, and shudders uncontrollably, convinces himself that he's cold. She curls into his side and wraps her thin arms around him. There's no face to stare at, just warm flesh pressing against his. She wriggles against him, pulls him on top of her, and in that brief instant, when he eases into the girl, her small hands gripping his arms tight like she's afraid to let go, he feels something strange like relief. But the girl is nothing like Sarah. His eyes adjust to the darkness. Her silence unnerves him; she's efficient and moves with a bloodless sigh. Her eyes bore into him, but he avoids her gaze. The crucifix winks in the weak light leaking in from the window. He moves in and out of her slow and hard, feels ugly with each lift of his hips and turns his face away, leans into the pillow, hopes the disgust in himself will fade. He holds his breath but is unable to finish, rolls off, and turns away from her. She lays on her back for a long time. He wants to apologize, to help her understand, to make himself feel better. He lights a cigarette. "It's been a long time."

She grabs his cigarette, inhales deeply, pauses, and exhales long toward the ceiling. Car lights flash across the window. In the parking lot, a man shouts, bottles break, more shouting. She sits up, flicks on the lamp on the nightstand, examines his face. "You look chock full of it." Her ribs poke out like slats. A large welt curls around her side. He touches it.

"Don't." She slaps his hand away; the nerves tremble on the dorsal part of his hand, prickling along the tops of his fingers. He holds out his hand, turns it over. He makes a fist; pain shoots through his wrist up his arm. The booze has worn off.

"Jesus Christ, you're all the same."

"I didn't mean to—" He touches her shoulder.

She slaps his hand away again. The pain tears into him like searing metal. By reflex, he reaches to hit her but stops himself, his open hand poised in front of her. He shakes out the heat until it thins, and his fingers go numb.

"Go ahead. Punch me." Her eyes blaze. "Go on, punch me." Her quickness surprises him when her fist smacks his face. He rubs his cheek. She punches him again, harder. "Hit me. Get it out of you."

His skin burns along his jaw, races up the side of his face, and for an instant he is tempted to slug her, to strike out and destroy what remains. He grabs her wrist and forces her to slap him again and again with the heel of her hand, and the sharp sting feels better than anything he's felt for a long while. He shouts out, "There, it's gone. Now what?"

"Sweet Jesus. You are all the same." She pulls her hand away and sits on the edge of the bed, facing the window. "I've got nowhere to go." She keeps her back to him, her voice a whisper.

The girl isn't going to last long at this. She'll be dredged up from the river come spring thaw, unrecognizable, bloated. His skin crawls to think what could happen to her. What did he think he'd do, save her? Talk to her about Sarah and his girls? He reaches for his jeans in a clump on the floor. Riffles through the pockets and pulls out the remaining bills, sets them on the night table on top of the phone messages. "This should get you through the next couple of days."

"And then what?" She wipes her eyes and nose on the sheet.

"You do what anyone else does. You carry on."

"Carry on?" She shakes her head sadly, steps across the room, her blanched skin stained black and red with bruises and welts on her back, thighs, calves. "If you don't mind, I'm going to take a bath to warm up before I carry on." As she passes the mirror, he notices the front of her body is scarred by more welts and bruises. The girl turns on the light and closes the door. She sets the toilet seat down. Moments later, the toilet flushes and the bath starts. He is surprised that the sounds comfort him.

He flicks on the TV. Polar bears lumber along the impossible white of the landscape. There's enough iron in their livers to kill any person who ate one. He doesn't know how folks figure these things out, but the part that gets him is one of the ways the polar bear hunts. It swims in the water alongside thick chunks of ice, covers its nose with its paw to camouflage itself, floating until it reaches an ice floe where seals and their pups lay. Some pups scatter into the water, some are unable to move quick enough. The attack is sudden and messy.

He lets go of the remote and stares at his hand, empty, older, tells himself there is no remote, there is no daughter's or wife's hand touching him, holding him. He counts out all five fingers with the other hand, picks up the remote, and clicks the TV to mute.

A few months before the car accident, he had walked along the river at the back of their property with the girls. The river had been frozen over. Five deer emerged from the timber. They stepped across the ice, lifting their black hooves high, setting each hoof down delicately, one after another in single file, hooves clicking on the surface. The girls heard the ice crack behind the deer.

"Daddy, they're talking!" Jody said.

But when the lead deer dropped through and thrashed around, breaking up the ice around it, she started to cry. He lifted her up and turned her away.

"Look," Christine said.

The other four deer paused and twisted around on the spot,

followed their tracks back to the river's edge, trotted a few hundred yards upstream, and crossed there. Christine and Kate grinned. Jody stopped crying.

"It must have been her time," Kate said. "Nothing she could do about it."

"Are they safe now, Daddy?" Jody said.

The deer jerked against the ice. He nodded.

"Promise?"

He nodded again. The deer flailed in the river, trying to get its hooves onto the ice to prop itself up; steam rose off its neck, its nostrils shrill.

"Yes." He set her down. "I promise."

She stared hard at him, her little brows wrinkled in disappointment. "I don't believe you."

They can never really be safe, no matter what we do to protect them. He knows that now.

Dwight rubs his eyes hard, knuckles digging into his sockets. He glances at the realtor's messages and considers a visit to the house; the girl can have this room for the long weekend. Maybe if he went back, stepped onto the porch where his girls played with their dolls, where Sarah and he sat late into the summer evenings watching the stars whirl in the vast charcoal sky, he wouldn't need to know what to do next, and he wouldn't be like some animal looking for something half dead to drag in.

The sound of the faucet rumbles in the bathroom; the girl coughs. He runs through the options. Drive to a neighbouring town, go shopping, get her some shoes and new clothes, pick up a bucket of chicken for the drive back, or let her sleep late, bring her coffee, watch TV together.

The taps shut off, and her body stutters as she slides in against the tub. A car horn honks outside, another bottle smashes. Then there's silence all around and he feels uneasy again. He peeks out through the curtains. The sky murky, fog hanging like cold blue smoke, low to the ground, the neon of the Northerner's sign faint. She could come to the house, sit in the truck while he checks things out.

"You're welcome to stay. Just don't expect me to hit you. Not till we get to know each other better." He chuckles to show that it's a joke. "So, what do you think?" He flips through the phone messages, crumples them, and tosses them to the carpet. He knocks on the bathroom door. Water splashes. His fingertips numb against the doorknob. "So, what do you think?"

"What's that?" she says.

He listens to the waves ripple, the drip of the tap, the supple pulse of her voice rising from the water. He holds onto the doorknob. On the back of his hand, the veins bulge next to the scars from when he punched through the ice to haul out the deer.

"Tomorrow," he says. "I was just wondering about tomorrow."

TRAVIS INSISTS THAT I have another drink. He's bragging about his conquests again and needs the audience that free drinks buy. Well into our second pitcher. The last round of neon syrupy shooters has blasted a hole in my brain. I've got an early start in the morning, but he's a pushy bastard. The new Aussie waitress spins into the dining room, three pizzas balanced in one hand. She props the door open with her hip, leans forward, and turns her head back toward the kitchen. "Are there any more clean plates?" she says. I'm a sucker for accents.

"Come and get it, baby." The dishwasher holds a plate in front of his crotch. Another greaser from out east, slumming it on his father's nickel, doing the boho thing, long hair tied back beneath a ball cap that reads *Dish Pig, Let's Get Dirty*. The waitress snatches the plate and strides into the bar.

"Dollars to doughnuts he's tapping that." Travis pours me another, lifts his glass. "This town. Christ. To easy prey."

The waitress sets down the pizza and plates, brushes a strand of hair out of her eyes, and glances our way. Travis raises his glass toward her. Every woman he meets is fair game; it's hunting season year-round. She smiles and ducks into the service area, lights a cigarette, and leans against the panelled wall.

"Check this out."

I turn to him. "Let me guess, you're going to marry her."

His mouth breaks into this shit-eating grin, teeth right out of a comic book, all bright and white and shaped like Chiclets. He grabs my neck and licks the side of my face. "I love you, man." He gets like this when he's drinking. People seem to think it's funny as hell, especially the women. I wipe my face with my sleeve. He holds up a hunting knife with a long wooden handle, snaps out the blade.

"Where'd you get that?"

"If you were paying attention, you'd know the answer." He turns the knife over in his palm and points it at me, carves a circle around my face. "The Bride. Last night." He jabs it hard into the tabletop where it quivers. He leans back, smiles. "Pay up, buddy-boy."

"Yeah, right."

He waves our empty jug at the waitress.

She crushes her cigarette into a coffee cup saucer and comes over with a third pitcher. "If you needed a steak knife, you could've asked."

That accent. I'd crawl forty miles over broken glass just to come home to that. A pink stone dangles from her neck, down between her breasts.

Travis grabs her wrist. "I was just making a point to my buddy. Why don't you join us when you get off?"

She yanks her hand away. "No thanks. I don't date psychopaths."

"Who said anything about dating?"

"Man, you can be such a jerk," I say.

"He's all mouth, no teeth. Harmless beneath all that B.S., aren't you?" She smiles, slaps Travis on the wrist and walks away.

"Mouthy little wench." Travis pours the beer. "Her ankles will be wrapped behind my ears by the end of the week. Guaranfuckinteed."

I'm tired as hell and look around the bar, map my escape route. The waitress bends over a table, picks up some plates and cutlery, her shirt tight on the curve of her waist.

"I'm telling you man, the Bride is crazier than she looks. She's pure butter."

"Butter?"

"Everything but her face." Travis laughs. "Seriously, she's got a little place in the Annex. Weird paintings on the walls. Gave me the creeps. And she's got this cat. Dude, she's crazy about that cat." He laughs.

I have no idea what he's talking about.

"She likes to hold it above her head when she's on top, gyrating and grinding like a belly dancer." Travis hunches forward, leans over the table. "Goddamn. What a night."

"Do you ever tell the truth?"

The woman has blue eyes that bore right through you like you were some unwanted dog coming in from a storm. We called her "the Bride" because she shuffled around town in a filthy, tattered wedding gown, sat in the doorways of postcard and T-shirt shops, sketching. Nobody in their right mind would go near her. She was a certifiable loon. "Was she any good?"

"She's got a good pussy." Travis laughs and punches me. "Pay up."

I dig into my pocket and count out five twenties, my tips from the last two days, drop them on the table. A dumb-ass wager; a hundred bucks for each girl we get in bed. The loser also has to sleep with her; if he doesn't, he pays double.

He folds the knife into its handle. "I couldn't leave without a little souvenir, could I?" He slips the knife in his pocket. "Now it's your turn. Let's see if you can rise to the challenge, buddy boy."

■

It was the start of summer holidays; I had just turned thirteen. My mother dropped me off at church. She gave me the choice to go with her, but it was hot out, and I didn't want to make the hour-long trip and wait in the pickup outside the bar while she drank and played the slots all afternoon.

In church, I held the hymnbook in my hands, mouthing the words. Across the aisle, a girl with shiny black hair that hung halfway down her back sang with her parents. I knelt on the flattened padding of the kneeler, pretending to pray, but most of the time I stared at my watch or glanced at the girl, hoping she would notice me.

After, I climbed up the riverbank to where Harley lay on the hood of his truck, squinting into the sunlight. "Boy, it might be Sunday but that don't mean you need to be so pokey." He rolled off the hood and opened the door. "Get in. We're running late." He had promised my mom he'd keep me busy over the summer at his buddy's place, a cattle ranch jammed against the border in the south country.

Harley drove fast, picked at his teeth with the corner of his cigarette package. I shifted in the seat against the door, stared out the window as trees gave way to open patches of bare land. We turned off the blacktop and drove the gravel.

"Learn anything at church this morning?"

"Yeah."

"What's that?"

"We're all going to hell."

Harley chuckled. "Amen to that."

The road snaked up through the valley above the river. Cattle stood scattered through meadows below the timberline and in clusters along the river. Harley drove with one arm on the window, the other on the steering wheel.

"You got a girlfriend?"

I shook my head.

"Why not. Good-looking guy like you. Lots of girls'd be interested. Anyone catch your eye?"

I shook my head and leaned my forehead on the window, gazed at the land rolling by through the side mirror. A cut line along the ridges ran east-west, the boundary between countries slashed through the forest like a thin scar.

"You gotta take what you can. Ain't no one give you what you want."

I felt him studying me.

"Your mom at work today?"

"Guess so."

"Don't cause her no grief, you hear? She's got enough on her plate."

"Yeah."

"Yeah, you understand, or just yeah?"

"Yeah, I understand."

"Good." He geared down, drove across a cattle guard. The vibration rattled through me.

■

The next night there's no sign of Travis; I feel obvious, sitting alone in the Northerner, pretending to read a paperback while watching the Aussie work the room. She glides between the tables, black curls bouncing on her shoulders, stops at an older American couple's table.

"Lemme try one of them elk burgers," the woman says, not lifting her head from the menu. Her husband sits with his thick arms crossed, orders a rye and coke. The Aussie glances back and gives me a bright mega-watt smile. She writes down their order and pours me a cup of coffee before heading into the kitchen.

After half an hour, the American woman pushes her plate toward the waitress, two small nibbles taken out of the burger, traces of ketchup smeared on the plate where the French fries were. "I ordered a beef burger."

The Aussie picks up the woman's plate, tells her she'll be back in a moment with a new order. The woman's husband grunts as he gets up and leaves the table.

"That's all right, honey, we've had enough. Just take it off the bill and we'll call it even, okay?"

When the Aussie hands the woman the bill, the woman picks through her change purse, holds each coin up in the fluorescent lights. "I don't know how y'all can tell your coins apart." Her husband waits outside, lights a cigar, and paces back and forth on the sidewalk. She drops a few coins on the table and leaves.

The Aussie clears their table and picks up the change piled

on top of the bill. Her shoulders sag. "Those cheap bastards."
She dumps the dishes in the service area. The clatter rings out
through the bar. She lights a cigarette, taps her foot nervously
against the wall.

I leave a ten-dollar tip for a cup of coffee and head toward her.
"Hey, looks like you could use a beer after work."

■

Harley and I got out of the truck. We walked across the yard
around the back of the barn to the trailer. A few men with duffle
bags hung around a couple of quads, and a boy, older than me,
perhaps sixteen, stood alone staring at us. One of guys stuffed
a duffel bag in one-two-three-four black garbage bags and
wrapped it in duct tape. Harley yelled to the other boy, "Hops,
get over here."

The boy walked over. Lanky, farm-tough. He had narrow
stony eyes and a vicious scar above his lip.

"Get him set up."

"Set up how?" He spoke slow, as if each word were an
inconvenience.

"Don't be a smart-ass. Show him around. Introduce your-
selves. Hell, I don't know. Sort it out. Be ready in ten, you hear?"
Harley walked toward the other men.

The trailer was oven-hot, stuffy. Hops fished a joint out of his
pocket. "Want any?"

I shook my head.

"Sure you do." He lit it, inhaled deeply, and held his breath for
a moment, studying me before letting out a low, long exhale, the
smoke pouring out of his mouth like a dragon.

Pencil nubs and topographic maps crowded a table with a deck of Penthouse Pets playing cards, and an ashtray overflowed with butts and roaches. Outside, through the filthy window, the sun burned high in a blank blue sky, the lodgepole pines blazed and shimmered. Cattle bawled, the murmur of men's voices, dogs barking. Harley chatted with one of the guys on the quad and tied down the duct-taped bags with bungee straps on the back rack.

Hops took another drag and tapped out the joint in the ashtray, slipped it into his pocket. "Come here, kid. I want to show you something." The quads started up and drove off; their engines buzzed like chainsaws. He grabbed me by the hair and pushed my head down, held me in front of him. He unzipped his jeans. "Open."

I try to shake my head free, but his grip was strong; he tore my hair, and I cried out. He clenched me harder. "That's it. Open up. Just like your momma does."

Hops seized my throat and squeezed. I thought this was it; this was how ends. I gasped for air and punched him in the stomach.

"Billy?" Harley called, reefing on the doorknob. "Don't make me break down this door." The trailer shook. I willed the door to snap off its hinge. "Goddammit, get your skinny ass out here."

Hops grunted and loosened his hold on my neck.

"I'm here," I coughed.

"Christ, you're giving me a headache. You got two minutes. Move it." The door stopped rattling.

I spat into an empty beer bottle where cigarette butts floated in stale beer. My eyes stung and my lips hurt. I turned away.

"Don't cry, little boy." Hops moved his fist back and forth in front of his mouth. "You're gagging for it, just like your momma."

■

The Aussie and I sit across from one another at the all-night diner. There's another cabbie in a booth and a lone cop, but otherwise the place is dead. She smiles, introduces herself as Linda.

I flip open my Zippo, drag it along my thigh to spark a flame, light her cigarette. It's a move I've practiced hundreds of time while waiting for the next fare.

"That's some trick." She tilts her head back and blows smoke rings.

"You're pretty talented." It's a lie, anyone can blow smoke rings. She laughs anyways; a good sign.

"It's easy. Pucker your lips, like this." Linda leans forward, her breasts push against the edge of the table. Her upper lip is moist. I swear, she could make cleaning toilets sound sexy. I try it and intentionally fail.

"It's okay, not many guys can handle a Zippo like you."

We laugh. "What's that?" I point to her necklace.

She holds it up in her palm, turns it over. "A rose quartz. A love gem."

"Does it work?"

"It gives me comfort."

She squeezes it and lets it fall against her skin and asks about me so I tell her stories and renovate my past so it might fit into her present and get her to come home with me. I tell her I'm saving money to buy a piece of land to build on before prices sky-rocket, want to open a drywalling business, start a family, get a dog, the whole nine yards. I'm not sure if any of these things are actually true. I haven't really thought much about my future, but saying it makes it real, as if I could somehow get there and live out my days in peace and contentment, whatever that means.

"You've always lived here?"

"Yeah."

She's silent for a moment, turns the ashtray in circles on the table as if she's considering asking me something important, likely about my childhood so she can get to know me better. I veer the conversation toward her and ask, "What brought you to town?"

"A postcard." She laughs. "Can you believe that? I remember thinking how beautiful it was. What I didn't know was I'd have to work all the time to make rent. I haven't even been out in the mountains, hiking or fishing or anything that involves leaving main street." She sucks on the filter and exhales. I've never seen anyone get so much out of a cigarette.

"It's harsh back there. The mountains aren't all they're built up to be."

She touches my hand and lowers her black eyes. Then she smiles, as if she's suddenly shy. It's not cold in the diner, but I'm shivering.

I look down at my plate, run my finger along the edge, and offer her the most honest line I've spoken all night. "Want a free ride home?"

■

We were out on the sun-baked dirt in the squeeze chutes, flanking the calves one at a time. Harley rammed the hot iron into their sides, and the stench of burnt flesh filled my nostrils; their spindly limbs kicked up dust. Some man who hadn't said a word all afternoon shot the calf with a dose of medicine, pulled out his Leatherman, and lopped off a chunk of ear, tossed it in the dirt where the heelers growled and scrapped each other for it. Hops kept the calf's neck pinned with his knee, laughing as the calf trembled.

"Billy, it's about time you gave this a try." Harley handed me a blade. "Hops, grab the front legs and pinch 'em tight." Harley and the silent guy tied the rear legs together, cinched the knot. To get rid of the bugs, Harley sprayed Muskoil and smeared a dark wash of iodine across the scrotum with a brush. "Now."

The calf lay stock-still. I held the knife tight, and despite watching them do it all afternoon, I couldn't remember where I was supposed to make the cut, top or bottom.

"C'mon, boy, don't pussy out on me now," Harley said. The calf jerked. "Cut it. Here."

"Fuckin' delinquents," the silent guy muttered. He crushed my fingers when he grabbed the knife from me, slit the bottom third of the scrotum, and blood shot out, splashed onto my arm. The calf bawled. The guy pressed his fingers along the sack until the testicles appeared like bloodied walnuts. He snipped the tendons of each, snatched my wrist, and dumped them in my hand, where they twitched in my palm, warm and sticky. He sprinkled a rash of powder on the slit and dusted off his jeans, a look of disgust on his face. Harley and Hops released the calf. It limped off, blood trickling down its hindquarters.

Afterward, over an open flame and beneath cold starlight, Harley fried them up. He spilled a stubby of beer into the cast-iron skillet, dumped in a beaten egg, a fistful of cornmeal, flour, salt, and pepper. "Here," he said.

I shook my head. All day I tried to keep clear of Hops, but he hovered nearby.

The hum of the quads drew closer; Harley wandered off to meet them. The heelers circled the fire, tongues hanging out, eyes glinting like embers. Hops plucked a testicle out of the skillet, shook Tabasco on it. "Not a word to anyone, motherfucker," he said, swallowing the glob with a smirk. "I'm all you've got."

■

Linda leaves the door to her basement suite unlocked for me on nights I work late. I take frequent breaks from my shifts and stop in to see her at the restaurant. I sit at the same table, near the service area, where I can watch her come and go, and we can share a quick smoke and talk trash about the customers. She's got a soft laugh, and when she leans over me to pour coffee, I can look down her white dress shirt at her lace bra. The rose quartz swings near the rim of my cup. She's got fabulous hips that sway side to side in tight black polyester pants, and when she flips her fleece sweater over her shoulder, waves goodbye to her co-workers, and reaches for my arm as we walk out into the cool mountain night, I'm part of something real, as if my presence counts in the world. She slides across the seat, places a hand on my thigh, and rests her head on my shoulder. Although I want to get to her place as fast as possible, I also want the moment to last. I take a deep breath of her hair and drive slow through the streets toward the river.

We sit on a flat, cool boulder along the riverbank, a blanket wrapped around our shoulders. I pull a beer from a six-pack hooked on a twig in a quiet back eddy and hand it to her. We clink cans and drink.

"I can't wait to get out of here," she says. "Make my cash, get on with seeing the real world."

I toss my beer can behind me, reach for another, crack it open. I've heard this talk before from outsiders. It's mind-numbing in its predictability. They have no idea what they're talking about, thinking life is elsewhere. I drink fast, want the beer to wash away the disappointment. Downriver, elk bugle, their screeches rise into the starlight. "Bet you've never seen anything like this before." I tip my can toward the river and trees and the outline of the mountains. "You said you wanted to get out of town and see the mountains. Well, here you are." I finish my beer and suppress the urge to burp, crush the can before chucking it behind me, and reach to grab another beer out of the river.

"What's that sound?" Her voice is quiet as if she knows she's offended me.

"Elk." I lob a rock in the river.

"Do they always cry like that?" She draws circles on my palm.

"They're calling out, challenging one another to fight for their harem of cows."

The screeches stop. Then grunting, muffled panting, an unsettling, primal sound, one you never get used to.

"How many cows?"

"Dunno. Lots. Twenty or so. They'd leave him in a sec if he showed any weakness. There's no loyalty."

She finishes her beer. The bulls wheeze and snort in the distance. Her body lays heavy and warm against me. "What about you?"

"Do I have a harem of cows?"

She kisses my chin, places her hand on my crotch, squeezes it. I feel myself harden and shift but she clutches me tight. "Are you loyal?"

I close my eyes and push up against her hand and hear her make a low sound in her throat. "I am now."

■

A week after the roundup, I was back in the south country. I had pleaded with Mom that I wanted to go with her to the bar, promised I'd stay put in the truck. But she was having none of it, told me how important it was to spend time with Harley. She said he was good for me, a real man of action.

Harley had Hops and me doing make-work jobs for Vince at the Last Stop 'n' Shop, spitting distance from the border. "I'll be back in a bit," Harley said, before speeding off on a quad toward the woods.

Hops and I stood behind the store, leaning against the wall. Hops sprayed some Lysol on Wonder Bread, stuffed it in his mouth, and handed a piece to me. The damp bread filled my mouth with a sharp taste like chemical apples and green jujubes. He squirted lighter fluid on the parched, knee-high grass around us. "Light it."

My face burned, and my hands trembled with the matchbox.

"What's the matter? No balls?"

"Quit screwing around, boys." Vince poked his head around the corner. "Pick up the garbage and cut the weeds." He glared at us for a long moment. "Ah, hell, get inside. I got something else for you two clowns to do."

"Chickenshit," Hops said. "Knew you couldn't do it."

In the back storeroom, Vince instructed us to sweep the floor and sort and stack old soft-drink empties in wooden crates. As soon as Vince left to attend to customers at the front of the store, Hops cracked open a bottle with his teeth and spit out the bottle cap; it rattled across the floor and disappeared under a mop and bucket. He drank the pop slow, his Adams apple bobbing as he swallowed.

"Making any progress?" Vince stood in the doorway, surveying the clutter. The shop door jingled. "It's a buck a pop, each. There's no handouts here. We'll make men of you yet." He walked to the front of the store. The door swung shut behind him.

"You got any cash?"

I shook my head. The bread was still glued to the top of my mouth. My stomach churned, and my head felt stuffed with wet cotton.

"Guess I'm just gonna have to fuck you up. Bad." Hops grabbed my neck and squeezed. I couldn't breathe; I knocked his arm away and massaged my throat. He held up the bottle and dropped it on the concrete floor.

"I hope that wasn't what I thought it was," Vince yelled from the front. "Four bucks and counting."

Hops held up another, dangled it between his thumb and forefinger. "You a momma's boy, ain't you?"

"Stop it." I tried to knock his wrist away but missed.

"I bet he's done time with Harley," Hops said. "Fucking low-life mules." He locked the door, lifted his T-shirt, hard ridges of scars twisted like knotted wood across his gut. He picked up another bottle half full of pop, held it up. "Your turn."

131

I tried to speak, but my tongue was thick.

"That'll pass," he said. "Remember to breathe."

I inhaled in short gasps. My head was fuzzy; the room blurred.

Hops laughed and nodded at my jeans. I shook my head but the motion made me feel nauseous. His hands reached to unzip them, the zipper a hoarse muffle that seemed to come from far away. He yanked my pants down with my briefs; they dropped like a heavy husk. The air was cold, and my skin felt bumpy and pebbled. I heard myself blurt out, "Vince," but Hops cuffed my face and pressed his palm against my mouth.

He swung the bottle and laughed, his face twisted and misshapen, flesh like plasticine. "You're royally messed up." He pushed me over a crate; the bottles clinked beneath me. I shuddered uncontrollably. He slid his thumb over the bottle top, shook it, and draped an arm over me, pulled me in tight. "Your momma would be proud of you." He jammed the bottle inside me; I cried out. He stuffed the neck in further until my stomach lurched and my insides felt as if they were pouring out of me. I was dry heaving, retching myself hoarse.

"Word is, your momma squeals like a pig," he said. "Like a stuffed pig. Just like you."

I tried to keep away from him as I dressed. He pointed to my shirt and laughed. It was on backward. I fumbled with my zipper, attempted to button my jeans. Vince's voice came from somewhere in the store, but I couldn't make out what he was saying. Hops shoved a mop in my hand and kicked a bucket toward me. "You're still gonna pay for the soda."

I pushed the mop hard against the floor, struggling to scrape it clean, to peel layer after layer of concrete off until I hit the clay beneath where I could tunnel furiously, dig deeper into the earth until the mud and dirt caved in over me, pulverized me into a speck.

■

It's a busy night at the Northerner, and Travis sits in my regular chair, not that my name is on it or anything like that, but since I've met Linda I've been coming nightly and sitting there, which pretty much makes it mine. He holds court like a wannabe alpha dog, chuckling with Linda. She slaps his forearm, leans toward him. His eyes drift toward her shirt, and he whispers something in her ear. She pulls away, smacks him on the thigh.

"Hey buddy-boy. Haven't see you for a few days," he says.

"Been busy." I grin at Linda.

"Your friend is a very naughty boy," she says, smiling back.

"Naughty is what naughty gets," Travis says.

He says the dumbest things. She laughs and floats toward the kitchen.

"Drink with me." Travis pushes the pitcher toward me. "She's something else, man. These Aussies are like minks."

"Yeah. They are." I regret it the moment I say it.

He looks at me. "Seriously?"

I glance around the room. Linda serves another table near the front of the bar. "Honest Injun." I hold up my palm.

He hands me a beer. "Well?"

"Well what?"

"You got something to show me?"

"Nope."

"No proof, no cash." He grabs me by the neck and yanks me

close. "I know you're bullshitting me, buddy-boy. Nothing personal, but there's no way you two hooked up."

He licks my face and laughs. Linda smiles at us, walks toward the service area. I turn to Travis. "Sure, whatever you say."

Afterward, I sit in my cab in front of the bar. People leave, leaning on each other. Someone kicks over a newspaper box. Another takes a leak off the curb, shouts at drivers who honk. A young couple grinds into one other against the door, laughs when the door opens, spilling them onto the sidewalk. A few nights ago, I watched a woman blow a guy in the backseat through my rearview, her blonde hair bobbing, the cab silent except for a low growl in the man's throat as he looked down, his jaw tight in concentration, admiring her work. I was grateful there wasn't much of a mess to clean up, not like the ones who vomit or shit themselves. These fucking people. No respect for place. I feel a headache coming on from the beer and lean my head back against the seat.

A little ahead of my car, the Bride glides down the sidewalk. She wears a black leather jacket over her dress. The tassels on her arms flap like strands of spaghetti. She makes a sharp, graceful turn and walks toward me, knocks on the window.

I lower it. Her mascara is pale blue filled with sparkles. Her lipstick atomic black. She points to my book. "Good?"

"Same shit, different characters."

"Story of my life." She leans into the window. "This must be the most boring job in the world. Drive people around and sit on your ass all night. I'd go crazy."

"It's temporary."

"Always is, honey." She opens the door. "Can I get a lift?"

■

Harley dropped me off again at the Last Stop 'n' Shop to chop down tall brush in the empty lot next door. Hops swore with each wild swing of the scythe. He glanced at his watch and stopped. "Ever seen a naked chick before?" He snorted. "Not counting your momma."

"Sure."

"Yeah?"

I nodded again.

"Yeah, right." He dropped the scythe. "Come with me."

"Harley will be back any minute," I said.

"Boy, you're none too smart, are you?"

I followed him across the open field to the edge of the bush where a ratty couch sat in a grove of aspens, their limbs bone white, flush with pale green leaves. The rich smell of topsoil and cattle drifted in from a nearby farmer's field. An old door rested on soft-drink crates for a makeshift table; a bald tire surrounded burnt coals and tarnished beer cans. A girl stood hugging herself. She had long black hair that seemed to glow in the sunlight.

"You didn't tell me you were bringing a friend," she said to Hops.

I turned away. The quad droned in the distance. I glanced at her again, certain that she was the girl I saw in church a few weeks back.

She scrunched up her nose, looked at me. "Do I know you?"

■

The Bride's cabin is an old garage converted into a living space, confirming what Travis had told me. I lean against the doorframe.

"Close the door. I've lost one cat to coyotes already." She turns the dial and finds a reggae station. "My wallet's somewhere around here."

Dozens of paint jars line the kitchen counter, mostly half-empty with various shades of blue and orange and black and yellow. Brushes poke out of another jar. Portraits on the walls. Human faces blurred by cross-sections of fruit, vegetables, fish. A man papaya. A child yam. A woman octopus. Two easels stand to the side. A plank of plywood spread across two sawhorses acts as a table, cluttered with books, fragmented shards of porcelain, pimento olive jars jammed with bright beads, packages of clay.

She turns on the bedside lamp. A black cat lounges on her futon, the bedcover a dyed piece of cloth. She lights votive candles sunken in painted glass containers with religious figures on each, covers the lampshade with a piece of red sheer fabric. The cabin darkens beneath a crimson glow and candlelight-flickering shadows on the walls.

"Place is a mess. I don't get many visitors. Sorry."

Something honest in her apology makes me feel warm toward her. I compliment her paintings.

"Yeah?"

"Yeah. They're really cool. You are what you eat."

"Here it is." She hands me ten bucks for the fare. "I'd say keep the change, but I need it."

I give her two dollars.

"They're my coarse attempts at mimicking an Italian master." She holds up a box of red table wine. "Drink? Only the very best for my guest." She laughs and pours two juice glasses to the top.

"To art." I drain my glass while still standing against the doorframe.

"Come in." She holds the box over my glass, presses on the nozzle, and fills it again.

When I push myself away from the door, the cat leaps off the bed and stretches itself against the concrete blocks of the night table. Its claws snag the drape of fabric, drags it over the candle, and the fabric bursts into flames. The Bride tosses the sheer on the floor, stomps it out. The cabin is hot, smoky, and she opens the window, waves a palette back and forth to clear the air. She laughs; I laugh with her and take off my jacket.

"That was a close call." She slips the wedding dress over her shoulders, lets it fall to the ground. The elastic edges of her black bra are frayed, and she's naked from the waist down, fanning herself, laughing. She has a thick, wiry patch of dark pubic hair that covers her crotch and creeps out from it toward her skinny thighs. Her stomach is small, but the skin is loose; she looks like a shrivelled prune, her best years well behind her. It's the saddest thing that's happened to me in a long time. The cat rubs itself against her legs.

I play along and drain my glass, holding it out for another drink.

She walks toward me carrying the box in front of her as if it's a sacred urn, swaying her hips slowly to the music.

■

"He's not my friend," Hops said.

He tossed the Aqua Velva cap into the fire pit, took a long swig, handed it to the girl. She made a face, held up her palms. He shrugged, handed it to me. I leaned my scythe against the table, pretended to take a gulp, and handed it back to him. He took another long guzzle and set it down on the door. Hops tried to kiss her, but she squirmed. He tried to kiss her again. She pushed him away.

"Do you live in town?" she said.

Hops sneers.

I nod. Her face is pale and her eyes are lost in dark shadowed hollows. Her throat moves when she swallows.

■

I slip out of bed and get dressed. My mouth is stale with spit and cheap wine; the bedside lamp glows. I walk around the cabin careful not to bump into anything and check out the paintings, but they are too big, too obvious. Search her desk, snatch a cluster of paintbrushes, set them down.

The Bride sleeps on her side, the sheets twisted around her body. Her thin breasts sag toward the mattress. Her stomach hangs loose in a wrinkled paunch. On the table I locate her purse, grope around in it, find a wad of crisp fifties, slip them into my pocket. She turns onto her stomach. I notice her stretch marks, realize she's some kid's mother, and feel disgusting. The cat is nowhere to be found.

Dawn breaks across the sky, splashes the mountain peaks with a scarlet glow. A couple staggers along the sidewalk, flags me down. I turn off my overhead light, speed past them. The man shouts, the woman flips me the finger. I whiz through the streets with the windows down; the rush of cold air washes out the cab.

The door to Linda's suite is unlocked. I turn on the shower

and use her toothbrush to brush my teeth. Her necklace lies on the counter with her makeup. I try to wash the Bride off me, spit out the toothpaste, gulp down hot water from the showerhead. I shampoo my hair and take the loofah hanging from the shower and scour my body until it tingles and burns. I rinse myself, stand for a long time under the hot water, then turn off the taps, towel dry, and clean my teeth again before sliding into bed. Linda shifts, mumbles, "How's work?" I hold her close, anxious that my body might betray me, whisper, "Busy night." My chest rises and falls against her back, and I focus on breathing slow, wait for sleep to come. I get a flash of the Bride, on her hands and knees, her cheek pressed against the wall, my fist clenching her hair. I feel myself stir next to Linda and press hard upon her. She doesn't move. I kiss her shoulder, but she doesn't move. I hold her tight, terrified that if I let her go, she'll drift away.

■

Hops grabbed the girl's hand and spun her around a couple of times. "Nothing like a good slow waltz." He winked at me.

"Stop it. You're making me dizzy," she said.

He pushed her down on the couch.

"It's dirty."

"We gotta get back to work," I said. The quad buzzed in the distance.

"Shut your trap." Hops ripped her T-shirt up over her head, tossed it to the side. He squeezed her plum-sized breasts through a small bra.

"Ouch. You're hurting me."

Hops twisted her bra strap, snapped it, laughed. "Off," he said.

She shook her head. He grabbed her hand and rubbed his crotch with her palm. "Gross. Stop it." She pulled her hand away and began to cry.

"Let's get out of here," I said.

■

The next day I find Travis at the golf course sitting outside the clubhouse on the patio overlooking the eighteenth hole patio. A Bloody Caesar sits on the glass table. The trees have turned, their golden leaves brilliant flares against their white trunks. Elk bugle in the distance; their shrieks float across the neatly clipped greens and fairways. Travis lifts his head. He wears sunglasses, his dark hair dishevelled. He reaches for his glass and holds it up. "Hail, Caesar."

"You look like shit." I feel refreshed as if the events of last night occurred last year. I'm good at forgetting quickly. I've had plenty of practice.

"Cheers, buddy-boy."

"To the Bride." I raise my glass.

Travis lowers his sunglasses. His eyes are bloodshot, weary. "Tell me you're joking."

I slap down the money I grabbed from her purse. "Drinks on our mutual friend."

"That's seriously cold, man."

"Pay up."

Travis chuckles. "Well, well, you're just full of it today, huh? Good for you. It's better than seeing you drag your ass around like some sad sack."

I lean back in my chair. The Lizard Range holds snow to the

tree line and soon will be coated in white. "What'd you do last night? Or should I say, who?"

"The usual. Northerner."

I laugh and punch his arm. "Didn't get lucky, huh?"

"Holding out on the Aussie."

"Not going to happen."

Travis stands, puts a hand on my shoulder, squeezes it. "It is going to happen. I'll double our bet. That's how sure I am." He counts out a hundred bucks and drops it on the table. "Enjoy the moment."

"Oh, I will." He walks through the restaurant and leaves. I order a drink and sip it alone. The narrow fairway slices through the valley beyond the green where men drive around in silent carts. Upriver, a bugling elk pierces the silence.

■

The girl shrieked, her thin arms crossed in front of her chest; she wriggled and twisted. Hops dropped down on her, grunting. She pried her arms free, slapped and punched him wildly, blue veins swollen on her neck. He pulled his jeans down with one hand, held her jaw tight with the other. She whipped her head side-to-side, snapped her teeth, but he leaned his forearm into her chin, muzzled her mouth with his elbow. Her face was contorted, red, unnatural, ugly; her eyes watery, pleading; her breath patchy, gasping sharply. The sunlight cut through the leaves and glinted off the scythe's blade.

■

Travis and I wait for Linda to bring us another pitcher of beer and when it arrives, he smiles slyly at her and she smiles back at him. I pour him a glass.

He licks my face. "I love you, man. Especially when you're buying."

I push him away. "I'll buy a lot more if you stop licking my face."

There's a commotion at the front door. A vaguely familiar voice draws near before I recognize it. The Bride stands in front us.

"Who the hell do you think you're fooling?" she screams.

"What are you talking about?"

"You fucking thief." Her face is red and her fists are clenched. She pounds the table. "Give it back."

"I don't know what you're talking about." I turn to Travis and chuckle.

Travis shakes his head and stares at the tabletop. Linda stands near the service area with a plate in each hand.

"You goddamn coward."

"Be reasonable. Let's sort this outside." I get up and try to lead her toward the door, but she swings her arm away.

"Be reasonable? You steal my money and want me to be reasonable?"

Travis shifts in his seat. I search for Linda, but she's nowhere to be seen. I dig in my pockets, offer forty dollars to the Bride. "I'll pay the rest tomorrow, when the bank opens. You've made your point. Just go."

"You're pathetic, you know that? Scumbag."

"While you're here, maybe you want to ask him for your knife?" It's a dumb-ass, cheap move, narking on Travis, but I have no choice.

"What knife?"

Travis stands and makes his way across the bar. I point at him.

"I don't know what kind of game you're playing," she says. "You're one sick asshole."

Later, at my place, I lie to Linda. She leaves it open for me, her fingers move up and down my forearms, her voice soft against my neck. I don't disappoint her. I tell her I drove the Bride home once and that she flirted with me, but I rejected her. That must be why she made the accusations. Travis slept with her, stole her knife, and bragged about it.

I stick as close to the facts as possible. It helps me believe the story myself, and I'm certain Linda believes it, too. It's easier to handle than the truth. I feel an unusual softness toward her, this unspoken pact between us, and I consider that this closeness will see us through.

She stops stroking my arm. "Thanks for telling me." Her voice is quiet.

I want to kiss her on the lips to confirm that my lie has worked, but she turns away.

"I'll walk myself home."

■

In the distance, I heard the quad stop and idle at the store, its drone crackling the air. Hops pried the girl's legs apart with his knees, yanked his underwear down, fumbled his hand between them. She cried out and reached toward me, her hand shaking. Her eyes turned toward the scythe leaning against the tree.

Vince came out of the store to meet Harley. Vince shrugged his shoulders, pointed toward the stand of trees we were in. The quad groaned to life and rumbled as Harley sped toward us. He stood and leaned forward, squinted in our direction, and hollered.

I grabbed the scythe, clutched it tight. Hops had his back to me, his jeans were at his knees, and his belt flipped back and forth against the dirt. I raised the scythe above Hops; the girl's eyes widened. The quad wailed closer, Harley's voice screeched in the air. I wanted to tell her that it's okay; it will all be okay, that it will pass, and you'll be fine. It might take some time, but you'll learn to slash it out of you bit by bit, leave it behind until maybe there's nothing left. Nothing left to do but survive.

As the hot grass swayed beneath us, I dropped the scythe beside her and sprinted out of the forest, away from Harley, away from it all, running as fast as I could, screaming at something, a past, a future, a life that seemed like no way out at all.

■

The dish pig informs me that Linda went home early. I buy a bottle of wine from the off-sales counter and leave. It's a clear, cold night; the walk energizes me.

Light seeps through her window. I peer through a gap in the blinds. Candles lit on the night table, the sheets a tumbled mess. Her hair is dishevelled. She sits on her bed in a housecoat. I tap on the window. Linda looks up; her eyes are puffy, but she doesn't move. I tap again. She doesn't move. I try the window; it slides open. She jumps back and shouts, "Get out before I call the cops."

"What's wrong? What happened?" I push the blinds aside but she looks scared so I stop from climbing in. "Let me explain."

"I'm calling the cops." She stands and picks up her phone. "You guys make me sick."

I close the window, leave the wine bottle on the sidewalk, and take off, running until my legs are heavy, my lungs tight. When I reach Travis's place, I bang on his door. I hammer the door again, lean over to catch my breath.

"Back here."

He's sitting on the picnic tabletop in the yard, beer cans strewn in the grass beneath the table. "Hey buddy-boy, what's up?" Travis smirks. "How's the Bride?" He sips from a can.

I charge him.

"Slow down, man. What the hell?"

I slap the beer away from him and soak his jacket.

"What the hell is wrong with you?" Travis sweeps the beer off himself and laughs. "Jesus. Chill. Have I got something to show you."

I grab his collar, twist, and pin him on the table. My first punch misses his face and slams into the table. It hurts like hell and only makes me angrier. "Were you even with the Bride?"

"What do you think, dumb-ass?" Travis sits up. "Christ, get it together." He shakes his head and laughs. Linda's rose quartz hangs off his neck.

My next blow hits him on the top of his forehead, thick and dull. Travis lays stunned, holding his head; blood seeps from the cut. I rip the necklace off and jab him with the pointed edge of the stone. He shoves me, and we fall off the table. He knees me in the groin. I curl up and cough; bile floods my throat.

"You okay?" he says.

I swing at him wildly but miss, get up and tackle him, slam

him against the table. We fall on the ground, and I pummel him with both arms, vicious punches that glance off his face and head. My fists are bloodied and sore.

He cries out; I strike him harder. Freshly turned dirt stuffs my nostrils. Travis knees me in the groin. I wheeze; blood and dirt flood my mouth. He struggles to get up; his breath is laboured, quick. He yells out. My eyes throb. I head-butt him, and a headache surges through me, a splitting pain that blooms and radiates through my skull. I rest my forehead against Travis's head and smash him hard again and again, smearing blood between us. His breath is shallow and rasps in my ear. I grab him, hold him tight, and sob against his neck, our chests rising and falling together.

BULL HEAD

WHILE SPLITTING WOOD one late October morning, Sonny sensed there'd be trouble when Bacon Face barked at his neighbour striding across the property, swinging a bucket of turnips.

The pail clanged against Bojan's thigh. Behind him, his glazed log home loomed wide and immense, its roof peaks vaulted toward the sky, a pre-fab package shipped up from the States. To the side stood a large pine tree with broad limbs that Sonny had climbed as a child while his father smoked his pipe below, and later where Sonny had hung deer, elk, and moose carcasses after hunting trips with his wife, Norma. "The Pines Bed and Breakfast" sign was now nailed to its bark.

Bojan's veranda sheltered cords of neatly stacked tamarack dropped off by someone Sonny didn't know. Sonny hadn't seen a guest yet, but suspected they'd show up in droves to escape the noise and pace of the city, relentlessly clawing away at their lives. They'd trample Sonny's property, snap pictures of the big pine or the gentle curve in the river, Bull Head Mountain in the background. They'd clutch their guidebooks and ask him about the upside-down mountain and then take pictures of his hand-chopped firewood, cords of it stacked in a convoluted system of woodsheds and lean-tos. Sonny planned to scowl when they pointed their cameras at him and Bacon Face, chase them away with his axe, shout like some wild man, laughing when he turned and walked back home, the axe across his shoulder. The novelty of it. Some people had no sense of place.

Bojan dropped the bucket at Sonny's feet. "What is this all about?"

Bacon Face circled Bojan, barking, his brown hackles up along the ridge of his spine. Sonny snapped his fingers and pointed to the ground where Bacon Face sat and growled until Sonny snapped his fingers again and the dog quieted.

Sonny crouched down and lifted another log. He couldn't understand what Bojan's wife, Milica, saw in Bojan, a crude rain barrel of a man who sounded ridiculous with his formalized English. He set the log on the chopping block and steadied it. "Looks like a bucket full of turnips."

"I am glad your sense of sight is not yet gone." Bojan shook his head from side to side; his grey whiskers scraped the collar of his plaid shirt. "Can you tell me why this bucket is full of torn turnips?"

Sonny picked up his axe, held the smooth handle in his palm. The head gleamed bright in the sunlight, sharp enough to slice the paper the annual property assessment was printed on. "No need keeping me in suspense."

"Just because you are mayor does not give you a right to joke at my expense. You know full well the reason these are shredded is that dog of yours. Milica is upset. Your mutt has been tearing up our garden every night."

Sonny winced at the mention of Milica. He lifted his axe and split a log. Woodchips dusted the sleeve of his flannel shirt. He stacked the wood against the white Tyvek-covered wall, bent over to pick up another log, and leaned on his axe. "I know we ain't been neighbours for long, but that ain't my fault. My father settled here in 1904. We've survived forest fires, two floods, mine disasters, disease, and every other affliction laid on this valley. If there's something we've learned over time, it's you can't tell which way the train went by looking at the tracks." Sonny stepped back, lifted his axe and struck the log, popping it in half. "You've got some nerve coming over here making accusations."

Bojan shook the pail in Sonny's face. "I do not care how long you have been here. A fact is a fact. Your mutt was in our garden."

"It weren't Bacon Face." Sonny dropped the axe. He walked over to the woodpile and grabbed a shovel leaning against it. He jammed the blade in the loamy soil of his garden, dug up a shovelful of turnips, shook the dirt free, and wiped them against his shirt. He placed each one carefully in the bucket. "Take these back to your wife. Let's move on and be neighbourly."

Bojan gripped the bucket handle. "If I see your dog sniffing around my property, I will shoot him."

"That won't be necessary. Even if he has wandered over there, and there's no way he did, I can guarantee you he's not interested in turnips."

"What kind of man names their dog Bacon Face?" Bojan turned around and trudged back to his house before Sonny could answer him.

■

Every day after chopping wood, Sonny walked to the Bull Head

Inn—City Hall, as it was known—a cramped bar with three guest rooms above it jammed with old refrigerators, broken neon signs, three-legged chairs and tables, and dusty, taxidermied bears, fish, wolves, and deer. Bacon Face followed, rooted around in the bunch grass and meadow parsley that choked the path. At the bar's entrance, Sonny picked up a log from the woodpile and pushed open the squeaky door, made his way to the woodstove. He tossed the log in, took his regular seat, and nodded to Lorne.

"Today's the day, Sonny. This will either knock your rubber boots off or melt them to your feet." Lorne set a bowl of baked beans in front of him.

Sonny picked around the beans with his plastic spoon and pushed it away. A jar of pickled eggs and another of pigs' feet sat on the bar top next to a rack of peanuts and Barney the Beagle, a taxidermy dog with a marble for one eye, once voted Mayor of Bull Head, his name embroidered on a toque that rested on top of his head. Lorne poured Sonny a cup of coffee. Sonny opened a *National Geographic* and flipped through the pages.

"Anything new?" Lorne said.

"Animals."

"What kind of animals?"

"Animals, dammit. Just animals."

"Who pissed in your cereal this morning?"

Sonny slurped his coffee and set it down. He kept his hand on the cup's handle, stared at it, rubbed it with his thumb. "Says he's gonna shoot Bacon Face if he goes near his property."

"Who?"

"Bo. Bohunk. Bojangle. However the hell you say his name."

"Empty wagons do the most rattling."

"Not in this case."

"He'll settle in. Look on the bright side. You're a shoo-in for mayor again."

Sonny lifted his eyes from his magazine. Five large jars crowded the faded red terrycloth tabletop. Above the table, pictures of previous mayors hung in a circle around a closed toilet seat with a caption that read: "Who's the next Mayor of Bull Head?" Anyone who lifted the seat found themselves staring into a mirror with an inscription, "You Are!" Sonny's jar was jammed with pennies, though he never put in a cent himself.

"I wish you'd leave me out of it."

"Hell, Sonny, even after you're long gone, we'll just stuff you like Barney, prop you up in the corner, and you'll still win."

Sonny shuddered. The annual election was something he used to enjoy, the media attention and film crews, the locals raising their glasses to him. It helped him forget Norma briefly. But when the crews left and the bar emptied, his longing for her returned with a searing vengeance. "Over my dead body."

"Precisely."

Votes in the form of pennies raised money for the volunteer fire department, established after the great fire of 1908. Anyone could vote as many times as they wanted, including the candidates, but whoever won had to promise that as Mayor of Bull Head, they would do absolutely nothing. The whole event rankled Sonny. It had devolved into a circus that only brought more people to town. Next to his jar sat the other half-empty jars of the other candidates: Ed the fly fisherman from Montana, Betty Ford, The Invisible Candidate, and Casey the Goat.

"It's no way to live out my days. Can't you just let things be?"

"Just don't lose to that one." Lorne gestured toward the Invisible Candidate's jar.

■

In his kitchen, Sonny dragged a match on the tabletop and lit a kerosene lamp. He pictured Norma smiling, handing him a cup of coffee. He blew out the match, dropped it to the floor where thousands of other matchsticks lay, turned down the wick, and placed the glass cover back on.

The light faded outside, the snags no longer visible on the mountain. Among the thick mossy stumps and thin second-growth, the concrete and brick skeletons of the coke ovens and powerhouse crumbled. Everything Sonny ever cared about was in those hills, and everything good was behind him. He pulled a tattered magazine from the stacks on his bookshelf and sat down in his father's old armchair to read. He picked up the matchbox and lit a few more matches, watched them burn to his finger-tips before blowing them out and dropping them on the floor. Outside the window, snow fluttered down. A shadow passed in Bojan's garden. Sonny pressed his forehead against the cold pane and peered into the darkness. "I'll be damned."

He sprinted toward Bojan's yard. Blue light flickered inside the house, but the porch was dark. Bojan sat staring at the TV in his living room. In the garden, Bacon Face dug furiously, dirt flying out behind him.

"Git. Go. Git now." Sonny pointed home and the dog bolted, his ears flattened, glancing back over his shoulder. Sonny kicked the dirt back into place and pulled away the loose roots, stuffed them in his coat pocket, and walked backward, careful to cover his tracks by smoothing out the soil and covering it with snow. He leaned against the tall pine to catch his breath and surveyed the garden. A crowded clothesline ran overhead from the tree to the porch. Wool socks, black briefs, nylons, a bra, towels, a pair of panties, a flannel nightie fastened by wooden clips. He heard a faint buzzing in the air. Milica moved past the kitchen window, her long grey hair loose on her neck. She entered the living room and handed a cup to Bojan, kissed the top of his head.

Something scurried across Sonny's neck. He swiped it away and placed his palm on the tree. It vibrated faintly. The bark was pockmarked with pitch tubes and frass and boring dust. More frass lay at the base of the tree. He slipped his pocketknife blade into the bark and sliced off a section the size of his fist. It fell away easily. He turned it over. Hundreds of round black beetles crawled over and amongst one another, gnawing into the wood. "Sweet Jesus."

There wasn't much old growth left, but Bojan's property was chock-full of second- and third-growth lodgepole and jack pine. Sonny checked them anyway, cutting away the bark and listening for the sound of chewing. He worked quickly in the dark, the snow falling thick around him, and checked one more tree. Satisfied there were no other vermin, he made his way to Bojan's house and knocked on the door.

Milica answered it, her hair now tied and held in place with a yellow pencil. Sonny fiddled with the doorjamb.

"Sonny. What a surprise." She looked past him into the darkness. "It's snowing. How beautiful." Her fingers were slender and clean against the grain of the door, the nails trimmed short.

He removed his cap and nodded.

"Come in. I'll get Bojan."

Sonny nodded again, wiped the soles of his boots on the mat. He heard Bojan from the living room, his voice moving closer until he stood in front of him.

"Are you here to bestow upon me an apology?"

Sonny held up the bark. "You've got beetles."

Bojan studied the bark, turning it over in his hands. Sonny stamped on a beetle that fell to the floor.

"If you're not careful, all the trees on your property will get infected one by one, and then they'll jump over to my place and spread across the valley."

"These little insects?"

"I'd be happy to fell that tree for you."

"Slow down. You are like a house on fire. Do you think I came over on the first boat?" Bojan's fists hung clenched at his side, the bark dangled from one of his hands. "Milica, can you believe what we are hearing? He wants to cut down our majestic tree." He pushed the bark toward Sonny.

Sonny turned it over to prevent the beetles from crawling on his hand.

"This is a dirty trick of yours to get more firewood," Bojan said. "Cut down your own trees. There are plenty of big ones left over there."

"This is serious—"

"Serious? Serious is what I was talking about this morning."

"That tree—"

"I have had enough. Now you must go back to your house and leave us alone." Bojan opened the door and motioned for Sonny to leave.

The door slammed behind Sonny. He stood in front of it for a moment, then turned and walked down the steps. Milica stood at the kitchen window. He tipped his cap to her but she did not respond.

At home, he shoved the bark in the woodstove and listened to the wood pop and fizz, the remaining beetles incinerated with a faint hiss before he shut the door and turned the damper tight.

■

Sonny slept fitfully and woke bone tired. He started a fire. The day was overcast and moody with bruised clouds, a skiff of snow lay on the ground. Milica's laundry line hung empty, her footsteps marking the snow below it. He sipped his coffee and tried to read. Each time he flipped the page and came to a picture of a tree, he wondered if it, too, had colonies of pests beneath its bark, eating away at its soul until it was too late and the tree had to be cut down, its long history ending in a heap of flames and ash.

He tossed the magazine into the fire, got up, and went outside to split wood. Sonny enjoyed the heft of the axe, smashing it down on a log, the fresh smack of wood in the air. It gave him a sense of purpose, the chopping and stacking and bringing in wood for the winter, and then later, during the cold months, the firewood keeping him warm. There was a satisfying self-made value to it that he hadn't been able to experience since he retired from logging.

Sonny selected an armful of dry wood and carried it to Bojan's house. He knocked on the door. There was no answer; he stacked the wood on the porch beside the door, and carried over three more armfuls.

■

"I'm saving my best just for you." Lorne handed Sonny a bowl of beans as he sat down with Terry and Neil. They had empty bowls in front of them and a fresh pitcher of beer. Sonny waved him off.

"I'll take it, if it's okay with you, Sonny." Terry stroked the ends of his moustache.

Sonny nodded.

"Hell, it wouldn't matter if it was moose steak and fried onions," Neil said. "He's not eating it. Not unless you threw on a dress and cooked like Norma."

Sonny glared at Neil.

"How's your neighbour?" Lorne said.

"Beetles."

"Christ," Terry said between mouthfuls of beans.

"What's he going to do?" Lorne said.

"Nothing."

"You sure?"

Sonny kept his head down, drew lines along the glaze on the wooden tabletop. "Too many of them crawling around town."

"Beetles?" Terry said.

"Goddamn strangers."

"It's a bit late to do anything about that, except blow up the ski hill or hope it don't snow for a few years and chase them all away."

"Can't make chicken salad out of chicken shit," Sonny said, wiping the tabletop. "That tree can't stay."

■

Sonny lit a few matches, snuffed them out; the smell of sulphur hanging in the air. He laid his palm against the windowpane. Bojan and Milica carried a cooler out of their house together, one at each end, stacks of blankets and pillows and two rolled-up sleeping bags on top of it. In the backseat, Bojan stuffed his shotguns beneath the blankets, walked back to the house, and locked the door. Sonny laughed quietly to himself; his own front door didn't have a lock. When his father had built the house, he'd declared that installing a lock would make his family prisoners of their own house. Milica climbed into the truck, slid across the seat close to Bojan. He lifted his arm over her shoulder and pulled her in close. She leaned her head against him, and they drove off. Sonny tapped on the window; his reflection stared back at him.

■

Terry and Neil stopped by the next morning.

"When they coming back?" Neil said.

Sonny set his axe down. "Couple of days. Maybe three."

Terry flipped open the tailgate and dragged out an electric chainsaw. He held it up above his head and grinned.

The men laughed. Sonny went into the shed and carried out his Husky 365, the filed teeth as sharp as the day he bought it, a gleaming twenty-eight-inch bar.

Neil and Terry unhooked the clothesline. Sonny yanked the choke, lowered his head, and listened for the saw to burp. He reduced the choke by half and pulled the cord twice before the saw started, the sound leaping out as he set it in the run position.

He cut out a V-shaped notch near the base of the tree and tossed it aside. The gap gave the tree a grim, toothless smile. Beetles shot out and scattered around the base. He worked along the side toward the back of the tree and made a clean back cut, letting the saw's weight do its work, slicing through a mess of beetle carcasses that flew out with the woodchips and sawdust, and stopped short of the face cut.

He paused. After hundreds of years, the towering pine stood with a thin hinge holding it upright. A beetle's head was jammed inside a pitch tube, its feet wriggling behind it in the air like some grisly cartoon. Sonny pressed his palm against the tree and pushed the trunk lightly, backing away as it began to fall. The tree crashed heavily, a tremendous echo across the property. Beetles ran frantically up and down its broad body. Neil hollered and clapped his hands. The men limbed the tree and bucked it into logs. Their saws whined in the air, and when they were done, they loaded the truck and checked the ground, crushed any stray beetles, and dumped their carcasses in the flatbed.

They drove the deactivated road looping up the mountain, past the remains of the boiler and tipple ruins, the mountainside around them pitted with holes and greening stumps left behind by miners and loggers, soon to be covered in snow that tourists would be skiing on. They stopped at a slash pile. Neil and Terry unloaded the tree; Sonny leaned against the truck and gazed across the valley toward his home, huddled against the bend of the river. Neil sprayed the pile with lighter fluid and lit it. Flames shot up and the wood began to crack and burn.

"What a waste," Terry said.

Sonny glanced toward the fire. As the flames flickered and

swallowed up the great tree, it shrieked like a dying animal. He turned away. His house sat below, small, surrounded by the woods beside a small meadow cleared by his father. Bojan's red metal roof glistened like a bright puddle of blood. A small gap where the tree they had felled was marked by the white stump. Sonny felt no joy in the aftermath. The pine had been standing long before anyone had first seen it, long before his father or the Kootenai. Sonny didn't need to count the rings. It took hundreds of years to grow, minutes to fell. Although he had lived here all of his life, the land had not softened; it was as hostile as the day he was born. He felt tired, a deep fatigue that a nap could not fix. He couldn't sleep most nights and thought if he did, he'd never wake up again. That would be all right with him.

"We're going to hell, every one of us." He climbed in the truck and waited for Neil and Terry to drive him home.

■

Sonny sat burning matches at the window when Bojan and Milica pulled up to their house. Sleet slanted in the twilight. They unloaded their truck, giggling with one another. The outline of a monstrous body lay slumped in the back, the head something awful and astonishing, its hulking rack weighed down on the tailgate. Bojan hauled the guns toward the house, stopped, set them down on the porch, turned toward the tree stump. He glanced around the yard, his forehead knitted in lines, and walked from one end of the yard to the other, as if the tree might have somehow been relocated or he had got his bearings wrong. His eyes narrowed into tight slits when he touched the fresh saw cut and smelled his fingertips. Bojan bent over to pick up a handful of sawdust on the ground, examined it in the palm of his hand, and squeezed it tight before flinging it down. He slapped the stump with the heel of his fist and shouted something Sonny could not hear. Milica hurried out of the house, spun around and scanned the property before she saw Bojan pressing his head against both of his fists on the stump.

She put her hand on Bojan's shoulder, but he shrugged it away. He struggled to stand and picked up a rifle. Milica took the rifle from him and set it down on the porch. She embraced him, stroking his hair, his shoulders shaking against her. She kissed the side of his head and his cheeks and held him tight. Sonny blew out the lamp and sat in the dark long after Milica helped Bojan into the house.

■

In the morning, fresh snow glittered on the ground, covering the axe rammed into the log and the loose chunks of wood scattered around it. Sonny sat inside, back from the window where he couldn't be seen. He kept his eyes on Bojan's house, but there was no movement.

At noon he walked to the Inn, Bacon Face trailing behind him.

He sat down.

"Have you heard the—"

Sonny held up a hand to quiet Lorne. He pushed his coffee aside and studied the tabletop. Lorne glanced up from time to time from his newspaper.

The door opened; Milica stamped her feet on the mat. She unlatched the woodstove, tossed a log in, closed it. Her arm brushed Sonny's. She nodded to Lorne, stopped at the election table, and surveyed the jars.

"I would like to nominate a candidate."

"Sorry, the race is already underway." Lorne shrugged his shoulders. "There's no more jars left."

Milica stared at Lorne and then toward Sonny, but he kept his head down. She looked at the jar of pickled eggs and the one that held a pig's foot and walked to the bar, unscrewed the lid, stuck her hand in the murky brine to lift out a peeled, glistening egg. She shovelled it into her mouth and chewed. When she was finished, she reached in and grabbed the remaining eggs, ate one more, and wrapped the last two in a napkin.

"This one is empty," she said, placing three one-dollar bills on the bar top. "I would appreciate it if you could wash it for me so I can nominate my candidate."

Lorne rinsed the jar, dried it with a towel. "Here you go."

Milica walked past Sonny again, the scent of freshly baked pie clinging to her. She placed the jar next to Sonny's, reached into her pocket, and dumped the contents of her change purse into the empty jar. She wrote "Bojan" on the back of a cardboard drink coaster and leaned it against the jar.

"Can I fix you a bowl of my world-renowned beans to help you celebrate?" Lorne said.

"No. Thank you. That will not be necessary." She turned to Sonny, her hair neatly tied back with a dark leather barrette. "You are a miserable, old, lonely man who bleeds ice water. You broke our hearts. I hope you are truly satisfied."

Sonny hung his head and picked at the table leg with his fingers.

"Please remove your wood from our porch. We will not accept your charity." She opened the door and pointed first at Sonny and then Lorne. "You people are all savages."

Sonny's face burned; he kept his head down long after he heard the squeak of the door close.

■

Sonny lay in bed unable to sleep, scratching his arms. Out on the porch, Bacon Face yipped in low gasps, half-barks punctuated by sharp breaths. Sonny looked across the room, out the window toward Bojan's house. He wagered the flannel nightie looked good on her. Bojan probably snored, kept her awake. That tree had to go. Would have destroyed everything around them all. He considered Bojan's ignorance, made worse by his awkward English. He lay back and closed his eyes, but he couldn't shake the sight of Bojan slumped against the tree stump, clinging to it, hollering into the night. Bacon Face's snorts died down until the night stilled. Sonny prayed for sleep to come.

■

Lorne asked if Sonny had seen the latest polls.

Sonny glanced at the election table cluttered with oversized jars, his full of pennies. Most of the candidates had significant amounts, except Bojan. Just the pennies Milica had left the previous day. A sliver of bark lay inside against the glass, and several beetles crawled over one another.

"Neil and Terry," Lorne said.

Sonny tapped the side of the jar. "Has Milica seen this?"

■

He could not sleep. His head droned with random thoughts, none of which Sonny could corral into a single coherent idea. He tossed and turned to relieve the itching on his arms and legs and imagined that the beetles were gnawing away at his house, crawling over his skin and burrowing into his bed, chewing his flesh. He slipped out of bed, got dressed, grabbed a heavy balled-up wool sock tucked away at the back of the dresser, and stepped outside.

The sharp air stung his face and refreshed him. Bacon Face lay in a tight curl on the doormat. He lifted his head. "Sshh, you keep put." Sonny took a deep breath through his nose and exhaled through his mouth, the fog of his breath a thin veil over the stars above him. He set off across his property to Bojan's house, studied the stump for galleries but saw none. No beetles, either. He went to a nearby tree, pulled out his pocketknife, and cut into the bark. The sap leaked out slow and dense. He smeared it between his palms, inhaled the musk of the old tree. His father had once told him that sap, like blood, is eternal. It courses through you like blood, it runs through the land; it was here before you were born, it will flow long after you are gone. Sonny buttoned his jacket against the cold.

The front door of the Inn was locked. He walked around to the back and tried a window, but it was fastened. He punched it with his elbow; the glass shattered the silence and crumbled to the floor. Sonny unlatched the window, lifted it, swung his leg over the sill, and climbed inside, his boots crunching on the broken glass as he waited for his eyes to adjust to the dark.

A streak of moonlight trickled in. He made his way to the

election table, grabbed Bojan's jar, and shook it. The beetles scattered about. He picked out the pennies and dumped them into his own jar, then carried Bojan's jar to the restroom, emptied the beetles into the toilet bowl, and flushed. Sonny tore his name off the jar and replaced it with Bojan's, sandwiched between the Invisible Candidate and Casey the Goat. He dug into his pocket and took out the wool sock, reached inside, peeled off five twenty-dollar bills, and dropped them in Bojan's jar, and then scrawled a note to Lorne about the broken window, instructing him to take what he needed to replace it, and to give the rest of the cash to Bojan. Sonny left the roll of money on the bar beside the stuffed dog, and climbed out the back window.

The night clear. Moonlight like buttermilk. Stars scattered like a pinch of salt. The snags and ruins on the mountain gleamed like ghosts in the forest. He'd kept his promise to Norma not to fell widowmakers; never considered he'd be the widower instead.

Bacon Face greeted him on his porch. Sonny lifted him, careful to use his legs to absorb the dog's weight.

"You're getting stocky on me." He backed into the door and pushed it open, carried the dog to the bedroom, and set him down on the bed. Bacon Face's tail tapped against the mattress. He rolled onto his back and squirmed back and forth, turned over, his tongue hanging out the side of his mouth, open in a strange grin. He sneezed and licked his front paws.

"Don't be getting too comfortable. This is a one-shot deal, okay?"

Sonny unlocked the drawer on his nightstand and slid it open, reached for a dusty shoebox fastened by rubber bands. They broke and fell away, the elasticity gone. He lifted the lid and pulled out a hand mirror with small jewels inlaid on its smooth back and ran his fingers along the teeth of the matching comb, set it down, and picked up the talcum powder. Unscrewing the lid, he raised the powder-puff and inhaled. The once strong floral fragrance was now musty. He sniffed it again, placed the powder-puff inside, and screwed the lid tight. He pulled out the silk handkerchief, unwrapped each of the four corners, and turned the hairbrush over in his palm where a few strands of long dark hair poked out. The filaments were soft and delicate between the pads of his thumb and forefinger, but he was afraid of breaking them and stopped touching them. He closed the drawer, the key jingled it its lock hanging from the hasp, and placed the mirror, comb, talcum, and brush on top of the nightstand, climbed into bed, and lay next to Bacon Face.

Sonny stroked the dog's side, ran his hands along the ribs, under his neck, scratched his cheeks, paused at his ears. He caressed them and breathed in the earthy musk of his fur, the rise and fall of Bacon Face's breath beside his arm, until they were breathing together.

The day before Norma had died, they had decided to leave their rifles in the camper and sat huddled through the pre-dawn cold in a tree stand, taking turns glassing for movement in the brush. Norma had noticed the bull first, looming like a massive shadow in the undergrowth, looking toward them but not directly at them. The rack was enormous. For a moment she thought two moose were standing next to each other. She kept her eyes focused on the moose; Sonny could almost hear her exclaim, *what a gorgeous creature.* She lifted the spotting scope, a wedding gift from Sonny, adjusted the focus, and pointed it at the bull and started counting silently. Sonny touched her knee, pretending to light a cigarette. She scuffed her boot on the wooden floor of the stand and lowered the scope. The moose raised his head, a trophy rack that had at least fifty points. It stared at them, majestic and terrifying and unblinking in its bulky beauty. Sonny estimated the rack to be about sixty inches across. He had never seen anything so stunning, so utterly satisfying in the calm of that moment before the moose bolted into the brush, its rack crashing a path through the poplars and aspens, laying waste a slaughter of branches and scarred trunks until the air was still.

Norma gasped and lowered the scope. Her eyes were damp when she turned to slap Sonny on the leg. "I hope you're happy. We're not going to get that close again this year, maybe never." She grabbed the cigarette from his lips and tossed it on the platform. "I wish you'd quit those things."

She climbed down from the tree and dashed ahead, glanced back, laughing, Sonny thought, although he was never certain. He tried to keep up, calling after her, anxious that the bull moose might still be near. She ran along the narrow winding game trail in front of him and jogged up a small rise where the trees closed behind her, their green limbs shivering in the grey morning light.

PIT BULLS

I

BRIAN WOKE IN the back seat of his battered Monte Carlo to the sound of dogs barking. The car reeked of ground coffee and stale sleep. He cracked the window to let in the chilly smoke of wood stoves from the valley, crawled over into the front seat to check his wallet, and prayed over the gas gauge.

Outside of his ex-wife's doublewide, a dog lay eviscerated in the grass, its jaw frozen in a grimace, eye sockets hollowed. Two ravens yanked at its innards in quick, vicious tugs. Brian dug in the ashtray, found a roach and lit it, inhaled, and held the smoke before exhaling through the gash in the window. The barking gave him a headache, but the pot shifted his thoughts. The slaughter of a prized dog upset him, but he could replace it; losing the money hurt like hell and would be much harder to make up. He peered over the steering wheel at the porch. Loveseat, wickered wine bottle with candle wax bleeding down the neck, tricycle knocked on its side—a gift for his boy's birthday bought before Brian's UI claim had been cut off. The glare blazed off the corrugated steel siding. Too much to look at. Junegrass lay snow-crushed in the honeyed spring sun. Frosted pine branch tips and rough fescue melted slowly, misting the air. Brownness everywhere wanting to be green, ready to grow after a long, punishing winter of shovelling rooftops and scraping by.

He scanned the twenty acres he had inherited from his grand-father and had the landscape memorized as if he were stand-ing on top of Buffalo Hump, the hummock that rose behind the trailer. To the east, the Elk River snaked along the bottom of the valley; to the south, densely packed forest thinned out near the border; across the valley, looking west, the runs on the ski hill scored the mountainside. Town sprawled out north of the property; far enough to be a dull flicker at night, a reminder of how good he had it here, tucked away from a life he could make no sense of, but close enough that he didn't feel completely alone. That was before he met Tracy. He wanted to raise chickens and hogs, plant a cash crop on the south slope, and build up on the Hump. But like most of his plans, they got lost in the dark details necessary to make ends meet, the shortcuts and half-baked ideas. In the end, the only way he could settle the child support with Tracy was to walk away from his birthright, the only land he had known, with a deal to lease back the chicken pens where he raised his dogs. Home sweet fucking home.

He pried open the glove box, grabbed the package of coffee he'd bought last night before he started drinking, and got out of the car. He nudged the dog with his foot, half expecting it to wake up. The ravens hopped off and squawked nearby. Despite being gutted, the dog felt heavy; Brian lifted the carcass by the hind legs and tossed it into the brush where the fescue and haw-thorn and antelope-brush coming in concealed it. He felt a faint rage seethe in his chest and punched the smooth alabaster trunk of a pine with the package of coffee. Don't be getting unhinged now.

Penny stopped barking and greeted him on the porch, yanked at the end of her chain, head and tail low. "Hey, princess." He crouched to stroke the top of her head, let her sniff his hand. She wagged her tail and turned so he could scratch her ear. The chain dragged across the wooden porch boards, ripped up paint that was already peeling. She was a year old and the female pick of the litter. He had wanted the male but couldn't afford him. At least with the female, he reasoned, she'd establish her reputation as a prized fighter and then retire early to breed. Then he could make some real cash. When he stopped petting her, she went back to her blanket at the side of the door. He tapped the screen with the coffee.

"Yeah," Tracy shouted from inside.

He stopped the door from slamming with the heel of his boot, edged it with his hip until it clicked closed behind him. "It's just me." The heavy smell of fried bacon hung in the air. In the living room, a mess of broken cups, lumps of wrapped clay. Two steel shelves buckled beneath the weight of unfired plates and bowls and jugs. On the coffee table, a half-empty milk glass, Saltines scattered in crumbs, stubbies, their labels ripped off in strips, a blue sippy cup. He picked up the milk and sniffed it, palmed the crackers, and shoved them in his mouth.

Tracy entered in her housecoat, towelling her long brown hair.

"Brought your favourite." He held up the coffee and tossed it to her. He wanted to tell her how pretty she looked, but instead pointed at the sippy cup. "What's he still using that for?"

She stopped drying her hair, bent forward, wrapped the towel around her head, then straightened herself. Her breasts strained against the housecoat. She was getting a little thick here and there and she looked pale, but sweet Jesus, she was a dime in a nickel town. He glanced down, and she drew the robe together tight at her throat. "Like you care. I'm sick of that barking all the time. Christ," she said.

"Anything else?"

She gave him a dark look. "You don't want to start in on me, believe me, today is not the day." She tossed the package of coffee on the counter and cleared the beer bottles. "You better bury that bloody dog."

"Buried it before coming in." He turned toward the sink, shook out the day-old grinds from the percolator, rinsed it out, measured out the coffee and water, plugged it in. As long as he kept his hands and eyes busy she wouldn't see that he was lying. He dried his hands. "Where's Junior at?"

"You really are incredible. Where do you think he is? In his room. He's still upset." Her tone stung like the slap of a palm.

The coffee burbled. "It's just a dog."

She studied him for a moment. "That's the problem with you. You'd jump over a dead horse to leave your son in a burning barn."

II

He stepped off the porch with a cup in each hand and walked through the brush behind the trailer. Chickens darted about the yard. It bothered him that she had turned down his coffee, something she had never done before. He clenched his cup tight and slurped from it.

A jute sack seared with the image of a moustached man in a

sombrero dangled from a motorized steel arm, swinging in arcs. Three pit bulls sprinted around the carousel. Two bitches chased the sack, churned up dirt and cedar chips, their rippled bodies taut as clenched fists. They squealed with each lunge at the sack. Sean was dressed in his usual—sunglasses, soccer cleats, spandex shorts, and a filthy Maple Leafs' jersey. Brian handed him a cup and saw his reflection in Sean's glasses. Small, unshaven, eyes narrow, hair flattened on one side of his head.

"What's up with her this morning?"

"She's not feeling well." Sean sipped his coffee. "Freshly ground, just the way I like it."

The red ran the fastest, her thick legs pounding the ground in a blur, the salt-and-pepper just off her shoulder. Behind her the stud lagged until Brian cut the switch. The two bitches leapt at the jute and tore at the man's smile. But when the stud bolted toward them, jumped up, latching onto the burlap, the bitches dropped to the ground, circled him with their heads low.

Brian smiled. "He's still got one more good fight left. Shouldn't have gone with Taz last night."

"It don't do any good crying over spilled milk. It could have been whisky."

"Maybe." He knew Sean was trying to lighten him up. The guy was easygoing, didn't seem to have any cares or worries, including the way he dressed himself. Maybe that's why Tracy fell for him. Or maybe Sean didn't have expectations.

"It cost me a fair chunk of change." Brian kicked the dirt and whistled. The stud unlatched and dashed to Brian's side, wagged his thin tail, and panted.

"Low on cash again?"

Brian kept his head down and stroked the dog's ears. "Don't say what you're wanting to say. It's too early in the morning."

"Hell, it's noon. And if I want to tell you to get a job, I'm going to tell you to get a job."

Brian looked up at the long vertical green scars and treeless strips on the mountain. "That hill's gonna be the death of this place." He coughed and shook his head.

"Lots of work up there."

"It's driving property prices up. Hell, I can't afford a proper motel room."

"Still don't see the problem." Sean wandered around the pen, his arms outstretched, feeling his way along the fence posts singing 'Amazing Grace.'

Brian winced. "You are truly butchering that song."

"I once was blind ... "

"Seriously, you need to shut up."

"... but now I see."

"Got me there."

Sean dropped to his knees, took off his sunglasses and bowed. "Oh Lord, I can see. I can see!" He stood and staggered around, laughing, and then stopped. "Seriously, I'm building a pottery studio for Tracy. I could use some help."

Brian surveyed Sean for a hint of sarcasm. "Worst part was seeing that goddamn Frenchy's grin."

"What kind of name is Jasmine? Christ, his momma must have loved flowers."

"I bet his parole officer would have something to say about his dog hobby."

"I'd pay you. Just don't tell Tracy. Are you interested?"

"Maybe." Brian had a vague recollection of Jasmine at the Northerner last night, buying shooters, sending one over, and winking before downing his shot. But what grated him was how Jasmine dominated the stage, singing one bloody awful karaoke song after another. His crude jokes and thick (or "tick") accent had the bar laughing and clapping for him. "Encore," they goaded. Brian smacked the dog's nuzzle hard. "Go on, git." He stood and faced Sean. "When do we start?"

III

They hauled lumber up the hummock behind the trailer and pens, a stack of two-by-fours between them. Brian's son, Brian Jr, carried a small bucket of nails. Sean poked an extra notch in the boy's toy tool belt so it would fit snug on his slim hips. After they dropped the lumber, Brian wanted to rest, but Sean turned around and trotted down the path. Brian Jr raced after him, belt flopping against his thighs. At the trailer, Brian rolled a smoke, lit it, and exhaled. "A cold one would set me straight. Got a head like a damn hornets' nest."

"Let's get the supplies up there first."

Penny barked. A pickup truck, its camper jostling side-to-side, entered the long, uneven drive and stopped. Jasmine turned off the truck, got out, and left the door ajar. His matted hair was tied back in a ponytail; his moustache drooped down both sides of his mouth. A dog sat alert in the front seat, its triangular head visible through the windshield. Brother to the runt that Brian had fought last night. The dog looked as menacing as its reputation; good stock, body shuddering as it sniffed the air.

Jasmine held up a crisp hundred-dollar bill and snapped it

between both hands, grinning. He spit on his palm and smeared the money with it, pasting it to the inside of the windshield. "It's yours if you want it. You just have to grab it." He wiped his hand on his moustache and glanced at his dog. Brian eyed the cash.

Sean whistled sharply, "Shut up." Penny barked once more and stopped. He nudged Brian Jr on the shoulder; the boy sprinted for the porch, flung open the door, boots clubbing the linoleum before the screen slammed shut.

Jasmine kicked the dirt as he approached them. He offered the hand he had spit on. Sean shook it. Brian kept his hands in his pockets.

"Rough night?" Jasmine said. "Shoulda brought him along slowly. Can't say I didn't tell you so."

Brian dug into his pocket and handed Jasmine a fistful of coins, a few crumpled bills. "That's all I've got."

Jasmine glanced at the money. "You're joking, right?"

"I'll have the rest soon enough."

"Do I look like a goddamn bank?"

"I'm good for it."

"I want you to understand one thing, you little pissant. I don't appreciate you yanking my chain." Jasmine whistled three sharp bursts. His dog jumped out of the truck and sprinted for Penny, leapt at her, and clamped down on her shoulder. She yelped and tried to shake him. Jasmine's dog lunged for her neck but tore her ear instead. She barked and rolled onto her side, but Jasmine's dog kept on, growling and snapping at her. Brian booted Jasmine's dog in the ribs and shouted, "Call him off." He searched the porch, found a Tonka Truck, and held the toy above his head. "Call him off, or I'll bash his face in."

"No need to get nasty." Jasmine whistled twice and pointed toward his pickup. His dog stopped, trotted back, its tail low, and hopped into the front seat.

Brian dropped the truck and examined Penny. The corner of her ear hung loose and bled. She nipped at him when he touched the gash. He felt around her ribs and neck and legs for blood, but found none. Tracy stood on the porch.

"Will you ever grow up?" she said. The screen door slammed behind her.

"Better take care of this." Sean followed her into the trailer.

Penny limped onto the porch and cowered beneath the loveseat. Brian turned to Jasmine. "That was a bullshit move."

"Honour your debt, or next time she won't be so lucky." Jasmine closed the door and started the truck. His dog leaned forward, head tilted sideways to see past the money pasted on the windshield. "Neither will you."

IV

"Let's get back to work." Sean picked up Brian Jr and put him on his shoulders.

They carried a stack of lumber up the Hump. At the top, Sean dropped the load so that it clattered on the ground. Brian jumped back so the wood didn't smash his feet.

"Wasn't my fault. You know it." Brian tried again. "Helluva place to build this thing."

Sean lifted Brian Jr from his shoulders and set him down. "Keep close." He handed the boy a small board and Brian Jr pounded nails into it with his plastic hammer. "Better here than our living room."

"Always thought it would make a perfect place for a house." The dogs barked down below, blue wood smoke curled from the trailer's steel chimney. Sean must have started a fire because Brian couldn't imagine Tracy doing so. Brian watched for movement at the kitchen window but there was none. Gunshots rang out from the firing range up the road. The wind rose, pushed the few scattered clouds out of the valley and high overhead, smearing the sky in a dull grey. Tracy stepped out of the trailer onto the porch in jeans and a loose blouse. Definitely gained weight in the middle. "She never once told me pottery was her thing."

"Did you ever ask?"

Brian winced and turned away. Tracy looked radiant now, the paleness from earlier gone, her face flushed. As she walked toward the base of the Hump, he knew that if she climbed up now, even if she stood beside him, she was there to be near Sean and the boy. He turned away. His son lifted a real hammer over a nail, stared vacantly at his fist. Brian gently held his arm back. The boy yanked his arm away and began to cry.

"Careful, you don't want to hurt yourself. Here, like this." Sean demonstrated with his thumb and index finger. Brian Jr stopped crying. He held the nail again with his fist and brought the hammer down on his hand and started to cry all over again. "No crying," Sean said.

Brian Jr sat with his knees at his chest, wrapped his arms around them, and rocked back and forth. It unsettled Brian; he was never sure why it happened or how to comfort him when he got like this.

"Everything all right up there?" Tracy said.

"Everything's fine," Sean said.

"Can't he learn nothing?" Brian said.

V

Brian unleashed the dogs in the pen while Sean ran after one of the chickens feeding in the yard. Brian pinched the salt-and-pepper's side, her ears, and her cheeks until she howled, and then he kicked her in the ribs. He kicked her again and felt himself get angrier. One good fight and he wouldn't owe Jasmine a nickel. The red bitch paced back and forth, growling. Brian loved her gameness. He squatted to call her, but she kept her distance, pacing from afar. She didn't quit or back down from anyone, and she'd rip his hand as he fed her if she felt like it. "Come. That's a good girl."

She skulked toward him. Brian kept his eyes locked on hers, reached into his pocket for a heart-shaped dog cookie, and held it out to her. "Sit." He offered the cookie; she snatched at it, sniffed the ground for crumbs, and watched him intently. He reached in his pocket for another cookie, and she wagged her tail. Her eyes shone with anticipation; he slammed her jaw with his fist. She reared, bared her teeth, and lunged for his leg. He kicked at her, but she dove for his leg again, ripping his jeans below the knee. He punched her again, chased her until his shirt clung to his chest, damp with sweat. She paced against the fence and avoided the corner, trotting along the sides so that when he approached she could dart out and make an attack. He had taught her well. She might be ready.

"What the hell's gotten into you?" Sean steered him away from the dog. Brian resisted, tried to shake himself free, but Sean's grip was firm. In his other hand, Sean clutched a chicken by the feet, it's head dangling and twitching. "Seriously, what's eating you?"

The dogs crept closer to the men, their eyes fixed on the chicken. The red kept her distance from Brian.

"Nothing."

"It's always nothing. Shall I do the honours?"

Sean tossed the chicken in the pen. It took off, running zigzags as the dogs chased after it. The chicken squeezed through the low fence rung, skittered back and forth in the yard, squawking. The dogs tore at the fence boards, ripped splinters of wood, moaning and squealing. Brian felt hungry and thought it would be good to have a home-cooked meal again. Tracy's chicken stew. A shadow of sadness passed over him.

"We're slacking on them too much," Sean said. "They're soft as poofsters."

"They're tired is all."

"They're worn out from trying to get to Penny."

Brian looked at him. "Speak plainly if something's bothering you."

"It's not easy taking care of all this." Sean shook his head. "She's in heat."

"What the hell are you talking about?"

"This. Everything. The dogs. I don't know." Sean moved his arm back and forth. "Fuck it."

"Nobody's holding a gun to your head."

"It'd be nice if you could contribute once in a while."

Brian heard the fatigue in Sean's voice and knew that Tracy had been pressuring him. She'd already insisted he talk to Brian about not sleeping out front in his car. Sean would hold out as long as he could, but she was a persistent woman. Brian took a deep breath, exhaled long and slow. "When's Tracy due?"

VI

The next day Sean and Brian hammered boards to frame the studio. Brian's arms hung loose and strong, and soon he established a rhythm of hammer and saw, enjoying the repetition, the go and flow, his favourite part of work, one he rarely experienced. The boy groaned, swatted at a mosquito on his arm.

"You okay?" Sean said.

Brian Jr waved off a small cloud of mosquitoes buzzing near his head. He stumbled backwards toward the lip of the hill, waving at them with his toy hammer.

Brian lit a cigarette. "Lemme show you a nifty little trick." He pulled his son away from the edge and blew smoke around his head and over his body. The mosquitoes flittered off, moved elsewhere. He considered telling him that this was the same thing his own daddy had once done to him, but he didn't. What was the use in that? Just confuse the boy. "Your mother won't approve, but this'll keep 'em away."

His son hid behind Sean. He peeked out and smiled. He hid again when Brian smiled back.

"I might have to take up smoking," Sean chuckled.

Penny barked. Music blared through the trees as Jasmine's truck jostled up the rutted drive. He stepped out of the truck, one hand on the open door, scanning the property, his dog sitting alert in the passenger seat. "There you are," he laughed. "Trying to hide from me?"

Brian shook his head.

Jasmine hiked up the side of the Hump, and a few minutes later stood in front of them, heaving over his knees to catch his breath. "Christ, building a fort up here?"

"A studio. For Tracy," Sean said.

Jasmine turned to Brian. "Thought she was your wife."

Brian's jaw tightened. "Old news."

Junior hammered, missing the nail each time, the dull thud of plastic against wood. Sean held a nail, demonstrated how to hit it. The boy glanced the plastic off the metal.

Jasmine rolled his eyes. "Might take a while at that rate."

"You'll have your money soon enough." Brian picked up a handsaw.

"I keep hearing that, but I'm not seeing it. Let me pick one of those bitches in the pen down there and we'll call it even."

Any one of his dogs was worth more than his debt. But there was only one dog he knew Jasmine would pick. The red. "You're off your rocker."

Jasmine stopped smiling. "I don't see many options. It's not like you're out there rustling the trees."

"He's working for me," Sean said. "He's good for it."

Jasmine stepped closer to Brian and lowered his voice. "There are consequences, *comprendes*? Consequences if you don't ... " He broke off and glanced at the boy. "Man up and honour your debt."

Brian gripped the saw. His son grunted, but Brian kept his eyes on Jasmine. He wasn't that big close up.

"Better reconsider what you're thinking." Jasmine nodded toward the boy.

Brian Jr banged the toy hammer against his own head. He tried to speak, but all that came out were strange sounds.

"He gets like this at times." Sean tried taking the toy hammer from Brian Jr, but the boy swung at him, laughing. "No sense to it." The boy resumed beating his own head.

"Doggie, doggie."

The saw's smooth wooden handle sat tight in Brian's palm, the heft of it light, the teeth jagged and crude. Jasmine wasn't worth it. Not here, not like this. Brian turned away and laid the saw down on a stack of lumber.

The boy gagged and sputtered, stared toward the porch, swung his hammer in the air. Jasmine's stud had mounted Penny and was pumping frantically.

Brian sprinted, found a shorter line down the Hump, and slid over the moss-covered rocks, branches tearing at his T-shirt. Jasmine lagged behind, taking the path.

Both dogs moved in a slow circular dance, until they stopped, locked and panting. Tracy ran from the porch. She grabbed the stud by its neck, but he turned and snapped at her. She cried out, clenching her wrist.

"Call him off," Brian shouted. He kicked the stud, but the dog remained stuck to Penny. He kicked it again, the blunt side of his boot smacked the dog's jaw. Both dogs whimpered.

"Christ, what a rodeo," Jasmine howled.

Brian reached for Penny's collar to pull her away.

"They're stuck, dumb-ass," Jasmine laughed. "Just wait."

The boy sat on Sean's shoulders, crying and banging his hammer against Sean's head.

"Is she all right?" Jasmine said.

"Hell no, she's not all right. Your dog wrecked her," Brian said.

Penny and Jasmine's dog stood locked, moving in a slow circle, whining.

"Not her, the little lady."

Tracy held her wrist tight against her stomach. Her eyes were damp and hard.

"Are you all right?" Jasmine said.

"Get off my property." Her voice cut clear through the air. "Both of you."

VII

Brian drove to the Northerner. Sean had been reluctant to give him an advance, but Brian used his I'm-good-for-it line. He knew it was getting stale, but how else was Sean going to respond? In the dim lights and faint stink of the cramped bar, a massive moose head hung on the far wall, draped with a string of multi-coloured Christmas lights.

Couples sat close to each other at most of the tables. A group of women crowded around a rectangular table beneath the moose head. An old man in a ball cap and gumboots drank straight from a pitcher of beer, his glass empty on the table. Brian took the table next to him. Another solitary old man wore a straw cowboy hat and a purple bandana. He sang "White Hot." His voice, slurry and thick, cracked on the high notes.

The women got up and danced together. Brian recognized them as hairdressers from a salon in town. They danced in a tight circle, giggled, each with a beer in one hand, cigarette in the other, glancing over their shoulders. No one approached them. It was too early in the night, and no man would do that to himself until later, when the music got louder and the alcohol had thoroughly erased his doubts.

The waitress brought Brian two high-tests. "He's awful, isn't he?"

Brian handed her a ten. "Least he's up there. Counts for something."

"Yeah, it counts for being a fool." She sighed. "I keep telling them to get that jukebox back in here. People want the real thing."

He wanted to point out that singing was the real thing, not the canned music thumping from a box in the corner of the bar. He wanted to ask her if she'd ever tried singing up there, but asking questions only opened the door to more talk, and he'd had enough talk for the day. He waved his hand when she offered the change.

"You sure?"

He nodded.

"Thanks."

The song ended, and the hair stylists stumbled back to their table, leaned into one another, laughing. One of them smiled at Brian. He fiddled with his tobacco pouch, rolled a cigarette. A few weeks after the wedding, he'd brought Tracy back to the bar and hoped she'd enjoy it as much as he did. She'd made biting, sarcastic remarks about the people who sat around drinking, playing the slots along the dark walls, or dancing like idiots. She barked a falsetto laugh every time someone sang karaoke. He never brought her back, and she never asked to come with him. He looked toward the woman, but she had turned to her friends. They lifted their shot glasses and then knocked them back, slammed the thick glass heels on the table.

Brian drank and ordered two more, drank those a little slower, waited for the buzz to seep inside him. He closed his eyes and listened to the old man sing, "Baby, I Love Your Way," his voice raspy and injured. Brian moved his lips along to the chorus. The music made him happy. He saw himself on stage and thought of Tracy, the anger in her voice; she always seemed mad at him, no matter what he did. Must be hormones. She was a raging lunatic when she was expecting. After the birth of Junior, nothing could get between her and the boy. Still the same. No room for anyone else in there. He didn't know how Sean did it.

A hand touched his arm, startled him. He opened his eyes; the hair stylist stood in front of him in a floral sundress and red cowboy boots. A heart-shaped locket dangled from her neck on a thin gold chain.

"Hey, wanna sing one together?" Her friends bowed their heads close to each other and watched him. "We could split the jackpot if we won."

"No. No thanks."

She pulled her hand away.

"I can't much sing." But that wasn't true. Tracy loved his voice. He used to sing Junior to sleep in the middle of the night during the first few weeks after he was born.

"It's just a song. I'm a terrible singer myself. We can share the pain." She giggled, touched his arm again.

"I never said I was terrible." The word hung between them like a bad note.

She slapped him on the shoulder. "You're funny."

He picked at the beer bottle label and sighed, leaned back in his chair. The old man neared the end of the song and Brian realized he had missed the best parts, the words he knew so well, the ones that reminded him of Tracy. What song didn't? "Sorry, maybe another time. I should get going. I have to work tomorrow." It made him feel good to say work, as though he had a legitimate purpose.

"Work, huh? Never heard that one before."

He got up to leave. Everything seemed to be turning on itself. Other men in the bar looked him over as he walked toward the exit, a strange hush between songs. He heard the women laugh as he reached for the door.

"Whoa, padre, where's the fire?" Jasmine pushed open the door and slung his arm around Brian's shoulder. "Was it something I said?" He laughed. "C'mon, let's blow off some steam. I know you're a shrewd businessman."

Brian searched his face for mockery.

"Have I got a deal for you." Jasmine steered them to the bar and ordered tequila. "For my *hombre*, *compadre*, burrito. Whatever. For my new business partner!" Jasmine raised his glass and downed it straight. "Go on, it's not gonna kill you."

Brian drank the tequila.

"You should be thanking me." Jasmine ordered four more shots.

"Thanking you? For messing up my dog?" Brian bristled. He had brought Penny along slowly, kept her away from the others, tied her up, and worked her into being a prized fighting dog. "I'll tell you what I should do is—"

"Your puppies to clear your debt." Jasmine raised his shot glass.

Brian set his glass down, drew circles on the bar top with it, studied the damp drawings.

"What use are inbreds to you?" he said quietly. There would be all kinds of health issues, deformities, nasty side effects; they wouldn't be good for fighting or breeding.

"What do you care? Those puppies will truly be gruesome creatures. You won't miss them." Jasmine raised another glass. "Deal?"

"I'm thinking."

"Not your strongest suit." Jasmine ordered two more, and when those were finished, they shook hands and celebrated with another shot. Brian felt lucid and lighter than he had in a long while. It's the booze, he reminded himself, though he knew the settling of his debt gave him this feeling. He could move on, start fresh, find more work, save, and show Tracy that he was everything she claimed he wasn't. He motioned for more tequila.

"That's the spirit. Partners," Jasmine said. They drank. The music bellowed and screeched from the jukebox behind Brian. He slapped the bar top with his palm in unison to the songs, and at one point he heard himself shout out, "We salute you," and saluted the hair stylist across the bar. Her friends pushed her forward. She strode across the room toward Brian, and he saw how everything, from the sheen on her hair to the fit of her dress and the glint of her pendant, was too perfect. She weaved in and out of the chairs, smiled when she dodged the waitress carrying another round for him and Jasmine. Brian pushed off from the bar, dragging his barge of baggage behind him, inevitable but unseen to her until she would get to know him, a time he knew would never amount to more than a night or two. And then he could cruise away, looking for the shore, never docking for long, staying buoyant for as long as he could manage. Jasmine grabbed him, his fingers digging deep into his shoulder, and whispered, "It must suck to know that your old lady's fucking him right now, in your home, with your retard son in the other room."

VIII

For eight weeks Brian and Sean punished the dogs, drove them to exhaustion until their bodies developed tight, gnarled knots of muscle that seemed to quiver when the breeze passed over them. Their noses twitched when the men came near, and their eyes were shining dark orbs that gave no real sense of the menace beneath them. Aspen buds popped and greened the stark limbs around the property; the warm air hummed with insects and birds. Penny's teats lengthened like thick pink worms, her sides filled out like a bloated sack.

Inside the studio, the men taped Gyproc while Brian Jr jammed his fingers in a small pail and scooped out gobs of mud, spreading it on a section of tape that Sean had stapled on a board.

"What the hell is Jasmine going to do with them?"

"Language," Brian said quietly, turning to his son.

"We won't tell Mommy, will we?" Sean grinned. The boy played with a fly caught in the mud. He ripped a wing off and watched it struggle in the muck.

Brian turned away. "Don't know. Don't care. Not my business."

"Christ, who knows how those things will come out, all disfigured and shit."

Brian Jr tore the other wing off the fly and then dug into the pail, plopped more mud on the tape. He stacked mud over the fly on the board, shaping a large mound over it like a grave.

"Not my problem," Brian said.

"Mommy, Mommy."

Sean stopped trowelling the wall and faced Brian, pointed the trowel at him. "If one of them inbreeds gets into my stock, I'm finished. Think about that."

"Your stock? Since when are they yours?"

"Since I fronted the cash and the space to raise them. Since I spend every spare moment taking care of them while you're fucking off wherever. Do you want me to go on?"

"Won't happen."

"It better the fuck not."

"It's a done deal." Brian wiped mud from his shirt.

Sean glared at Brian for a moment longer before he lowered the trowel so that Brian Jr could slap mud on it.

"Fuck not, fuck not," the boy said.

IX

Brian found Penny in a cramped space beneath the porch. Her stomach rose and fell as she panted; her eyes calm, dilated. He snapped away the lattice and laid out a blanket for her, but she paced back and forth, dug frantically. She abruptly lay down trembling. Her stomach convulsed in spastic jerks. She stood, paced again, and vomited. Brian nudged a water pail toward her.

"Drink some of this. You're going to need it."

She lay down again and stared at him. He lit a tailor-made and smoked until she started to contract. He knocked the ash off the cigarette on his boot heel and carefully inserted it in the package with the others.

The first puppy slid out a few minutes later, a damp plop on the blanket. Penny chewed away the slimy membrane, licked the hairless pup from top to bottom. Brian sliced the umbilical cord. Penny lay breathing heavily, ignored the pup struggling on the blanket. She strained hard again and the next three came out tail end first. Her pauses were longer now; tiny nubs of bald flesh surrounded her, gnawing at her teats, soft muffles in the straw. The fifth one came out slow and motionless. Penny bit the membranes away but stopped before she was done. Brian placed his palm on the pup. It was warm and wet and lay motionless. He pulled his hand back quickly, pushed it aside with his boot. "Had enough?" Two more struggled out.

"Beautiful, isn't it?" Tracy stood behind him on the porch. She touched his shoulder. "Sorry, I didn't mean to startle you." Her wrist was scarred from Jasmine's dog; she held a cup of coffee. "Here, looks like you could use it."

Brian took the cup, sipped from it. "Your hand okay?" Her belly seemed more distended up close. He turned back to the puppies so she couldn't see his damp eyes.

"Yeah, Sean fixed me up."

"He's a good man."

"He's got his moments."

Brian wiped his eyes and looked up at her, pointed his cup at her stomach. "Why didn't you tell me?"

The clatter of crickets clawed at the edge of the property. Soon it would be dark, and he'd leave for town, the bar, and then sleep it off in his car. He wanted her to soften, face him with eyes that smiled back at him.

"What's there to tell?"

She had a point. Her future stood in the way now, one with Sean and his son and another on the way. He wasn't a part of it anymore.

"I suppose you're right. Congratulations. It'll be good for Junior to be an older brother." He turned to the pups. They wriggled over each other to latch onto Penny, blind, bonded through their need to be warm and fed. They looked all right, nothing strange about them; four paws, two eyes, two ears. Once Jasmine got ahold of them, the puppies wouldn't have a chance. Not much of a world to bring them into.

Tracy crouched down, took turns stroking each of the puppies. "They're amazing. So helpless. Miracles of life."

He closed his eyes and listened to her low voice, to the puppies' murmurs and their soft paws on the blanket, to the crickets in the distance, and for a moment he felt stillness.

"For better or worse." He stood. "For better or worse."

But Tracy wasn't paying attention to him as he walked toward his car, the yips of puppies drowned out by the hiss of twilight, flooding the sky like a purple bruise.

X

Brian found Tracy on the porch each morning, playing with the puppies. He would wake up in the back seat of his car and hear her voice, low, cooing. He'd lie there, close his eyes, and imagine Tracy speaking to him, tracing the outline of his collarbone with her fingertip, the palm of her hand on his neck. She used to lay her head on his chest and tell him to shush so she could listen to his heartbeat; she'd close her eyes and lie there smiling. He felt himself stir and closed his eyes tighter, tried to block out the daylight that seared through the windows, but it was no use; it would be minutes before Sean showed up and started banging on the front hood of the car.

He got up and climbed the Hump to work with Sean and Junior, snuck glances at the porch down below.

"Somebody die?" Sean said.

Brian listlessly sanded the drywall, aware that the work on the studio was nearing completion and that he'd have no excuse to stay anymore. Junior tore a sheet of sandpaper into small pieces and tossed it in the air like corroded snowflakes, waved his arms up and down.

"I'm not here to entertain you," Brian said.

"You've been hanging your head about all morning. Yup, I'm entertained. Having the time of my life." Sean grabbed his side and let out a mock chuckle.

"Tamed, tamed," the boy said.

"Your silly-ass garb entertains me every single day." Brian coughed. "When's the last time you played soccer or hockey? Never known you to play."

Sean let out another mock laugh. "That's a good one. Stop, you're killing me." He straightened himself and thrust out his chest, held his head erect. In an unconvincing English accent he added, "You don't need to play to be a student of the game."

"That's the corniest, stupidest thing that's come out of your mouth today."

"I am who I am." Sean stretched his arms out. "Like it or lump it." He crossed his arms over the maple leaf on his chest. "You see Jasmine yet?"

Brian shook his head. "This whole thing would be a non-issue if I made an anonymous call to his parole officer."

"Like hell." Sean stroked the top of the boy's head. "You'd end up getting us all busted and come away with nothing. You don't think Jasmine will talk? Christ. He'd sing like a canary."

"Not like I've got anything now." He watched Tracy below, holding a puppy, snuggling it close to her face.

"Look." Sean pointed at the dog pen behind the trailer. The stud swung from the jute, his jaw locked, his body tight and gabled like woven rope. "He's ready. You have a chance to get back to making some serious cake."

"That'd be nice." Brian picked at the window frame, flicked slivers in the air. Tracy bent over the porch and re-emerged with another puppy.

"Christ." Sean glanced at the boy, but he was preoccupied with picking up the shards of sandpaper he'd discarded. "Why can't you just ask?" Sean dug into his shorts and handed Brian a rumpled wad of bills without counting them. "Money goes through you like a sieve."

"I don't need your charity."

"It ain't charity. Consider it another advance."

"Clarity, clarity." Brian Jr had stopped picking up the sandpaper and was now smashing pinecones against the doorjamb.

Brian put his finger to his lips to hush the boy. "She's getting on with them." He nodded down toward the porch.

"Don't I know it." Sean picked up Brian Jr and put him on his shoulders. The boy leaned back to look at the sky.

"Has he seen them?" Brian said softly, nodding toward his son.

"Was I born with a hole in my head?"

XI

Brian woke with less of a hangover than he had expected. They had finished painting the studio the previous night. He squinted into the light, the tops of the aspens and firs swaying in the breeze. The green trees, the blue sky, the vivid world above. Tracy spoke in low, hushed tones to the puppies. He sat up and looked at himself in the rearview mirror, cleaned the sleep from the corners of his eyes, and combed his hair down. He slapped his face a couple of times and got out of the car.

Tracy sat watching the puppies play amongst themselves. Brian placed his boot on the porch and leaned on his knee. "I thought there were six," he said, his voice low in her ear.

"There were." She sniffled with her head down. "You know how it goes." She pointed to a mound of dirt in the flowerbed marked by a cross fashioned from two popsicle sticks tied together with a few strands of long grass.

"I can't afford to lose any more."

He heard her sigh. She wiped her nose with her sleeve. The puppies crawled and tumbled over one another. He turned away. The aspens and poplars were flushed in bright green leaves, their smooth white trunks a contrast from the coarse black trunks of the firs. Inside the house, Sean's voice, Junior laughing.

"I appreciate you volunteering to help with my studio. You didn't have to do that." Tracy held up a sock. One of the puppies tugged at it.

"No problem." He leaned close to smell her hair again.

"Our son is growing up fast." Another puppy joined in on the sock.

Brian felt encouraged by hearing her say "our son." Something they shared, something they created together, something to always bind them together in the future. "You've done a good job with him."

"I've had a lot of help," she said.

Sean and Junior chanted something that Brian couldn't make out.

"They're like two brothers together, you know?" Tracy smiled.

"It's nice being around here. Seeing him, you, the dogs."

She lifted her head. Her eyes were a deeper, softer brown than he had remembered, and he felt an understanding so strong, he was sure she was thinking the same. It seemed impossible that they had not made their marriage work. He could not see his future, and he imagined her life as nothing but emptiness even though she had Sean and Junior. He touched her shoulder and turned her toward him. Her face was tense, drained of colour; the lines around her mouth tight; he wanted to apologize, to set things straight. He leaned to kiss her. She turned away. Junior chanted at the screen door, a chewed-up giraffe dangling from his hand. He pushed it open. Sean stood behind him.

"Honey, that's Penny's." She grabbed the giraffe and tossed it into the brush. The boy started to cry.

"Come on, little man, let's go back inside." Sean turned Brian Jr by the shoulders, but the boy wriggled against him.

Brian made a face, hid his eyes behind his hand. His son cried harder. Brian turned his hands into small circles. He viewed his son through them, smiling. But he saw Sean instead, glowering; the boy screamed and punched Sean's leg.

"Come here, honey." Tracy opened her arms and hugged Brian Jr. She ran her hand through his dark hair, straightened out his bangs, wiped his nose with her sleeve. Junior squirmed against her, turning away from Brian. She held his son close, kissed his neck, rocked him.

"He's hungry," Sean said.

"Do you want some macaroni and cheese?" she murmured into the boy's neck.

Brian Jr nodded.

"Can you get the water started? I'll be there in a minute," she said.

Sean paused at the door, turned around and glared at Brian, and then disappeared in the trailer.

"I need you to never do that again." Tracy's eyes narrowed. "Do you understand?"

Junior pulled away from her and squatted in front of the litter. "Puppies, puppies." He slapped the soft head of one.

"Careful," Brian said, his voice barely audible. "You don't want to upset the mommy."

Tracy picked up their son. "We'll talk about it inside with your father." She turned to Brian. "You can't hang around here any-more. It's confusing for the boy, it's confusing for you." She hurried inside, the porch door slammed shut behind her.

Brian stared at the puppies and listened to Junior scream, "Puppy, I want puppy." Sean and Tracy spoke, but he couldn't make sense of what they were saying. His son continued to scream, "Puppy. Please. Puppy. Please." Brian pressed his hands hard over his ears. The puppies squirmed helplessly at his feet.

XII

He drove to the Northerner, ordered two high-tests, and sat

down. He drank resolutely, ordered two more, drank those as fast as he could, and belched to himself.

The old man sang "I Walk the Line." Tonight he wore a bright orange bandana and black felted cowboy hat with a feather poking out of the side. When the old man finished singing, Brian banged his beer bottle on the table. A couple sitting nearby glanced at him and turned away, shrugged their shoulders at one another.

The old man stopped at Brian's table. "'Preciate it, son." He handed Brian the song list. "You're here most every night. No question you got a song or two in you."

Brian picked at his beer label until the bottle was bald. "I've got to have a few more of these first."

The old man put his hand on the bottle. "Go on, no harm in trying. Next round is covered."

Brian flipped open the binder, ran his finger through the song list. The songs blurred one after another until he came to a song he used to sing to Tracy when they first married.

"Go, on. Give it your all. I'll keep an eye on things."

"Lord knows I've got nothing left to lose." He finished his beer and carried another, shoved the binder under his arm, and muttered to the DJ, "24-B-11."

He stood on the empty dance floor where he and Tracy had sung their song after exchanging vows in the church. Sean had clapped wildly, grinning ear to ear, in his tuxedo and soccer cleats, and bellowed, "Belt it out, buddy. Shout it to the mountains." And he did, singing himself hoarse as he lifted Tracy, twirled her around, watched her laugh, hair falling across her eyes, caught in the corner of her lips, spinning around, her veil, her mouth, a tumbleweed of laughter, the future careening toward them faster than he imagined, one he was not ready for: the mill closing down, Tracy pregnant, Junior's hooded eyes. Brian left town to work in the Interior, and on his days off he stayed behind in his motel room rather than going home to the screaming, nonsensical boy and his wife, crazy with it, telling Tracy that he was earning overtime on the weekends, a story she believed for the better part of a year until she showed up at work one day with his son in her arms, clutching a stack of unpaid bills, and the crew boss informed her he'd fired him months ago. By the time Brian returned home, Sean was there and handed him the papers to sign; she didn't want to see him again.

He waited as the refrain began. The Dobro rose, the fiddles rose, Willie's sad song rose, opening up and beckoning him before falling in a steady rain of sound over the beating of his heart. He took deep gulps from the bottle and looked around. The old man tipped his cowboy hat and Brian felt a surge of gratitude for him, nodded back. On the other side of the room, Jasmine leaned against the bar and toasted him with a shooter glass.

"It must be my lucky day," Jasmine shouted. "Wouldn't miss this for the world, partner."

Brian cleared his throat and picked up the microphone. The words streamed across the bottom of the monitor faster than he expected, colouring from yellow to pink before he could form the sounds. The first stanza passed, and he heard the couple sitting nearby snicker. He waited for the next line, and when that scrolled by, he lost track of the words, confused by the music he knew so well. His faced burned. Fear moved through him slowly, as though he'd swallowed it, and by the time he braced himself for the next line, it came and he missed that, too. The old man leaned forward, coaxed him, mouthed the words. Brian dropped the mic to his side. Jasmine's laughter rose over the music.

The old man took the mic from Brian. "It happens to all of us. You'll get over it, and you'll try again and you'll do a great job."

Like hell he would. Brian hurried through the bar, his eyes down.

"Nice work, partner," Jasmine said.

The waitress offered him a shooter, but Brian kicked the door open and was greeted by a slap of cold air.

As the door closed, Jasmine said, "I'll drop by in the morning, pick up my pups."

Brian drove fast, hit the gravel corners hard, slid out of them with soft swerves, fishtailed to right the car, mesmerized by the ease with which the car floated over the rutted straightaways of the road. The sky greyed to the colour of ash, faded fast to charcoal. He pulled into the driveway, turned off the ignition, and sat listening. A few dog barks from behind the trailer. Whiskey Jacks and magpies chattered in the aspens. On the Hump, the studio's light glowed soft from the windows, music floated down, carrying Sean and Tracy's laughter. Junior sat on Sean's shoulders, and they chased Tracy around inside the studio. Brian reached in the glove box for a builder's pencil. He tore the lid off his cigarette package and scribbled, "I'm costing you too much. Sorry." He leaned over the back seat for a jute sack, clicked the door handle open, cold metal against his palm, and stepped out into the cool evening.

The air became silent, and the grass seemed to cower at his gaze. He slipped the note against the screen of the porch door. When he reached Penny, she stared warily. The puppies slept against one another, squirmed against her side. Brian stroked her head, whispered her name. She licked his hand, her ears relaxed. One of the Whiskey Jacks blurted out, bursting the silence with a long sorrowful cry that rose above the trailer.

Penny stood and snapped her jaws when he reached into the pen and scooped up two puppies, dropped them in the sack. When she snapped at him again, he slapped her face hard, knocked her back, stunned. He snatched another puppy by its velvety neck and dumped it in the sack. He couldn't stop himself; the puppies were finished no matter what, forced into a life where they'd fight and lose, and never measure up. Penny lunged at him, bit his arm, tore the flannel cuff. He slugged her, fished out the last two pups, warm and soft, their legs peddling the air, urine dribbling down one of them. Penny clawed at him and clamped on his arm again, opened a gash. Blood seeped through his shirt.

"You'll get another chance."

He slung the puppies over his shoulder and hurried to his car, tied the top of the sack in a simple knot, and dropped it on the ground. The sack jostled with cries; dime-sized paws and doughy limbs pushed against the rough burlap. He climbed inside the car. His eyes stung. Listening to the murmuring cries of the puppies, he sobbed deep in his throat. On the Hump, the studio seemed to pitch back and forth, an electric air that vibrated through him. He started the car, put it in reverse, and stepped on the gas. The crunch of cartilage rose from the ground, beneath the tires, travelled violently up into his stomach. He retched and shouted out, slipped it into drive, and lurched forward. Reverse. Drive. Reverse. Drive. He felt crazier with each thump of the gearshift until he stopped, slammed it into park, and cut the ignition.

Penny howled from the porch, her tail erect, a hoarse rasping wail piercing the air.

Brian got out of the car. The sack lay motionless, soaked with blood; the thick smell reminded him of rancid milk. He snapped open the trunk, dropped the sack inside, banged it shut. He tried to wipe his hands on his pants, fumbled for a cigarette, lit it, inhaled, and coughed heavily, held a finger to one side of his nose and blew. Then the other. His sobs doubled him over. He shook the string of mucous off his finger. Can't get it right. One disaster after another. The studio loomed above. They were up there, living their lives, going about their business like all families do. It seemed impossible that he shared the same world as them. When he stood up straight, his heart was lighter, but his head throbbed and his eyes burned. He got into the car and started it.

The night bled in around him. He drove to the gravel turnoff where the main artery led toward the dull lights of town. In his rearview, brake lights blazed a trail behind him. He took his foot off the brake, turned in the opposite direction, and accelerated, keeping his eyes on the road as it unfurled a few yards ahead in the white wash of the headlights. The wilderness rushed toward him in the glow, trees flashing past like an ancient chorus in a cold cathedral. The car swerved, gravel peppered the undercarriage, dust obliterated the road behind. He crushed the gas pedal to the floor; the cruel rush of night air stung his face like a slap. Brian turned off the headlights and sped faster, the wind screaming in his ears as he lifted his hands off the steering wheel, and hurtled through the darkness.

Acknowledgments

There's no one I'm more grateful for than my wife, Nancy Lee, for believing in me and for blessing me with her strength, beauty, and grace. Hot on her heels, of course, is our puritanical office manager and little funny buddy, Jaine.

A special thanks to my family, especially Annie Vigna, and Mark and Peter Vigna. Daniel Sarunic, Nancy Chen, and Dave and Monica Ilett. And to the Lyin' Bastards: Judy McFarlane, Sally Breen, Dina Del Bucchia, Keri Korteling, Carol Shaben, and Denise Ryan for their guidance, bottles of wine, celebrity gossip, and numerous pieces of cake.

I've been fortunate to have generous, perceptive readers who have seen some or all of these stories at various stages, in particular Keith Maillard who encouraged me from the beginning. Much gratitude towards Calvin Wharton, Steven Galloway, Charlotte Gill, Chris Offutt, Todd Craver, Adam Honsinger, and Andreas Schroeder. A shout-out to my peers from UBC and Iowa.

Anne McDermid for her unflagging support. Francis Geffard for being the first to jump on board. Peter Oliva, Kevin Chong, and Cathleen With for their sage advice. The Banff Literary Journalism Program, particularly Moira Farr, Ian Pearson, and Rosemary Sullivan. Shirley Dunn and the Dave Greber Freelance Writers Award.

I'm appreciative of my colleagues at Douglas College and the University of the Fraser Valley.

And I'm deeply grateful to Brian Lam and the rest of the enthusiastic team at Arsenal Pulp Press.

JOHN VIGNA'S fiction and non-fiction has appeared in numerous newspapers, magazines, and anthologies including *Cabin Fever: The Best New Canadian Non-Fiction, The Dalhousie Review, Grain, Event, subTerrain*, and *The Antigonish Review.* He is a graduate of the MFA program at the University of British Columbia and alumnus of the Writers' Workshop at the University of Iowa. John lives in Vancouver with his wife, the writer Nancy Lee.